Good Night Diary

Life, Love And Everything In Between

Alex Griffin

Disclaimer

Please be aware that this book contains descriptions of mental health issues including self-harm. For a more details description please see relevant websites or seek help from a professional.

Contents

Dedication

Tracey Adkins is the most inspirational and creative team member.

A Hope Creator but also a gift to everyone

About the Author

This author's name is Alex Griffin. He is a young author who has Autism, and he didn't know he had autism until the beginning of his adult years. So, most of his work is written from his autistic perspective, which gives a unique edge to his work and writing. Not just the stories he creates but the emotional impact his works bring to the reader. Also, his happy and energetic personality

Introduction

Hello, today marks a fresh start, a new chapter in my life. I, Felix Jones, have decided to take control and document my journey towards healing, hence this diary. It hasn't been an easy road, but I'm determined to leave my struggles with mental health behind and embrace a brighter future. This diary will be my companion, a safe haven where I can pour out my thoughts and track my progress. I got this diary as a Christmas present from my sister, Mary Jones; it has sat on my shelf for months so let's make the most of this.

I spent most of my life, we'll all of my life in a small village in England just outside of London called Elltbridge, where everyone knew everyone and secrets were hard to keep. It was a busy village street of brick houses nestled next to parks. The noise of the cars intertwined with the barks of the dogs. There were a few shops and a local village coffee shop, which was always over-ornate. It was always a dysfunctional village, but it was a place I could call home.

Secondly, I go to the school in the village, well everyone does who lives here. Elltbridge Grove School was a fairly large school filled with multiple hallways with classrooms left, right and centre. When I first started at Elltbridge, they gave everyone a map so we wouldn't get lost however, we all did. At school, I had a best friend, well he still is called Tommy.

We have been friends all the way from preschool, so he describes us as Batman and Robin or Joey and Chandler. Tommy was a hilarious friend and could brighten anyone's day just by looking at his infectious smile. He was the school's rugby captain and also charming, so he was instantly a popular boy. Actually, he has led Elltbridge to win the state school's rugby championship two years running now and is trying to make it three in a row. Most days after school before my mental health got bad we would hang out in my room after school playing card games, such as Poker. This is while we gossiping about school drama. Just to mention I would win most of the time. Tommy only lived the street next to mine, so practically neighbours. I never told Tommy what I was going through because I felt I couldn't tell anyone. As my mental health got bad and I would distance myself from him, I think he knew something was wrong, but he never knew, even though he would have been so supportive and told someone so I could have got the help I needed. I bet he just thought that I was stressed about upcoming exams, which our happening once school starts up again in a few weeks.

Growing up, I always felt different, like I didn't quite fit in. As in my early teenage years, the dark clouds of anxiety and depression began to loom over me, casting a shadow on my once vibrant world. The struggles in my everyday life, from family issues and the constant bullying at school, I was being bullied for my weight and being different. I struggled to understand these emotions and ways of feeling, often feeling alone, misunderstood, and unworthy. The bullying was a few boys who were also on the rugby team with

Tommy. I am not going to get into details about the bullying, but it was horrific, something that no one should experience. Tommy and my family never knew about the bullying, as I thought it was the only way to stop it. Everyone at Elltbridge says "Snitches get stitches".

My parents loving and supportive, tried their best to help. They provided me with every resource they could find, but sometimes, it's the demons within that are the hardest to battle. It was like a bull in a tether. Out of me and my siblings, I found myself retreating into my own world, becoming a master of hiding my true feelings. I put on a brave face, pretending everything was okay when, in reality, I was falling deeper than anyone could have imagined.

My sister Mary has her own apartment now, a good drive away with her boyfriend. I don't get to see her often since she's always caught up with work, puts in long dedicated hours to her job and is often seen juggling multiple tasks. She has recently found solace in baking, which has occasionally led to the sweet treat entering our household. Most of them were edible and actually delicious. I could not have asked for a more loving and supportive sister.

On top of that, I also have a brother, Jace. Jace is similar to me, as he is a little shy and is unique. He is studying and living in the big United States of America on a rugby scholarship. This means I only see him on special holidays such as Christmas and summer times.

We both have different tastes in things; he likes his taste to be modern and trendy, while, I like classic and a little vintage (one of a kind). I could wear a sweater vest all day long, in my opinion, they are comfy and customisable.

I should tell you who is in my family vine.

I should tell you what happened before I carry on. The turning point came when I reached my late teens. I had hit rock bottom, and finally, the weight of my struggle became too heavy to bear. I would hide away from the world, confiding in self-harm to reduce stress;

however, looking back at it now, it only made things worse. In my mind, by scaring myself felt like a coping method to stop all the feelings inside. Now, the scars are part of me and a burden I will carry for the rest of my life. The marks I have created within the body tissues where the sores I made will never fully heal.

I would spend all of my time in my room because it was a sanctuary, a place where I was alone with my thoughts and no one could influence or hurt me. I love my room; my parents let me decorate it how I wanted, two tall white bookshelves filled with fantasy stories from faraway places. I also had a TV, which sat on top of a family antique storage unit. I think it was my great-grandmother's. My large bed was so comfy; It was like sleeping on a cloud made of marshmallows. On my window sill, I had photos of me and my family when I was younger. On my twelfth birthday, my father bought me a large green fluffy rug, which to this day is the centrepiece of my room. The rug matched my long, drapey curtains. Attached to the side of one of my bookshelves I love to place posted notes with quotes for books that I have read and thought meaningful.

I have talked way too much about what has happened. This is meant to be a new chapter in my diary. I couldn't quite articulate: sadness that felt like an unwelcome guest, anxiety tightening like a vice around my chest, and the overwhelming urge to inflict pain on me as a desperate measure to regain control. But that evening, I knew it was time to share my truth with my parents the very people I had tried so hard to shield from my inner turmoil.

As the sun dipped below the horizon, casting a beautiful yet haunting twilight glow over the brick houses., I called my parents to the living room. My mother entered first, her smile fading as she noticed the serious expression etched on my face. My father followed, his brow furrowing with concern. The air felt thick with unspoken words, each second stretching into eternity.

"I need to talk to you," I began, my voice barely above a whisper. My palms were clammy, and I could feel the weight of their gazes probing me, searching for reassurance that everything was alright. But everything wasn't alright, and that much was clear.

"What is it, sweetheart?" my mother prompted gently, her eyes glimmering with concern.

Taking another deep breath, I gathered the fragments of my bravery. "I've been struggling… with my mental health. And I don't want to hide it anymore."

Their expressions shifted a mixture of confusion and worry washing over their faces. I continued, words tumbling out in a rush, spilling the secrets I had kept locked away for far too long. I talked about the black clouds that often loomed over me and the suffocating weight of despair that made it difficult to get out of bed some days. I watched as my mother's eyes widened, her hand unconsciously reaching out to rest on mine, a silent promise of support.

"I also, sometimes hurt myself," I admitted, my voice cracking. "It's like a release, a way to feel something other than this numbness."

I slowly pulled up the long navy-blue t-shirt underneath my sweater vest, revealing multiple scars just above the elbow. Silence engulfed the room, and the world outside seemed to pause as I braced for their reaction. My father's face paled slightly, the reality of my struggles hitting him hard. But there was no anger in his eyes, only sorrow the palpable ache of a parent witnessing their child in pain.

"Why didn't you tell us sooner?" my mother asked, her voice a whisper filled with concern. "We could have helped you."

"I didn't want to worry you," I replied, tears spilling over. "I thought I could handle it on my own."

They moved closer, forming a protective barrier of love around me. My father spoke next, his voice steady though laced with emotion. "You are not alone in this. We will find help together. You don't have to shoulder this burden by yourself."

I let their words wash over me, a balm for the wounds I had carried in silence. I felt a flicker of hope ignited within me for the first time. I wasn't just a person struggling in the dark; I was part of a family, and they were willing to walk alongside me through my darkest moments.

"We love you," my mother added, wrapping her arms around me, and pulling me into a tight embrace. "We're here for you, no matter what."

As the evening wore on, we talked about seeking therapy and ways to cope with my feelings. I felt lighter as if the heavy stones I had been lugging around were finally starting to fall away. We may not have all the answers, but together, we will navigate the difficult path ahead.

In that moment, as I sat with my parents, surrounded by love and understanding, I realized that vulnerability wasn't a weakness it was a courageous act of self-love. And for the first time in a long while, I looked toward the future with a glimmer of hope, knowing that healing was not just a solitary journey but one we would embark on together. Spending the evening in bed reading a fantasy book after just telling my parents about my mental health struggles

After spending the evening in bed reading a fantasy book from my extensive book collection, I felt a sense of calm and escape from my thoughts. The magical world in the book allowed me to forget about my mental health struggles for a little while. It was a much-needed break from the stress and anxiety I had been feeling.

Telling my parents about my mental health struggles was difficult but I knew it was important to open up and seek support. Their understanding and reassurance made me feel less alone and more hopeful about the future. Sharing my feelings with them was a step towards healing and getting the help I needed

Good night Diary!

Day 1

Dear diary I am going to write this diary, the day after telling my parents everything, which is today. Now I have written about my past and why I am writing this diary, let's start today. The sunlight streamed through the sheer curtains of my bedroom, casting delicate patterns on the floor. I squinted at the clock on my nightstand at 8:00 AM. The memory of the previous evening, when I finally mustered the courage to tell my parents about my mental health struggles, loomed large in my mind. Their expressions had been a whirlwind of concern, confusion, and love, and I wasn't sure how I felt about what had transpired.

I'd spent countless nights feeling as though I were wearing an invisible cloak of sadness, my heart heavy with the weight of unshared thoughts. The effort it took to speak those words aloud the truth about my anxiety and depression had been monumental. Yet, the relief of finally opening up had been intoxicating. I had expected their reaction to range from disbelief to disappointment, but what I got was something far more profound. They were quiet, taking in my words, and then they wrapped me in their arms like a safety net.

Now, sitting up in bed, I wondered what today would bring. I pushed aside the covers, noting the coolness of the wooden floor against my bare feet. As I padded to the kitchen, I heard my mom's familiar humming, a soothing melody that made the house feel warm and alive despite the uncertainty that hung in the air.

"Morning, sweetheart!" she called, her voice bright. I stepped into the kitchen, where the aroma of freshly brewed coffee enveloped me like a hug. My dad sat at the table, a newspaper spread out in front of him, but his eyes were fixed on me instead of the headlines.

"Hey, how are you feeling this morning?" Dad asked, his voice laced with an underlying worry that cut through the joyful chaos of breakfast.

"I'm okay," I replied, my own smile feeling slightly forced. I reached for a mug, pouring myself the coffee my dad had already prepared. It was strong and bitter, just the way I liked it. I took a sip, savouring the warmth as it settled in my chest.

Mom set a plate of toast adorned with overcooked eggs in front of me, her gentle touch lingering longer than usual. "We were thinking. maybe we could do something together today?" she suggested, glancing at my dad for support. "Just the three of us, you know? Spend some time outside?"

The thought of being outdoors made my heart flutter with both anticipation and anxiety. I loved nature, but my desire to escape my mind often clashed with social situations. My gaze shifted from mom to dad, who nodded encouragingly, his eyes filled with encouragement.

"Yeah, that sounds good," I replied, choosing to lean into the idea.

After breakfast, we donned our jackets and stepped out into the crisp fall air, the sun dazzling through the trees. The three of us made our way to the park, golden leaves crunching beneath our feet. I noticed how gently they held my hands as if they were aware of the fragile nature of my feelings.

As we walked along the winding path, I found the courage to share more. "I've been feeling really overwhelmed for a while," I said, looking out at the ducks gliding over the water. "Sometimes it feels like I'm drowning, and it's hard to keep my head above water from all the bullying."

Mom offered her hand, and I intertwined my fingers with hers. "We're here to help," she said softly. "You're not alone in this. We want to understand more so we can support you better."

I took a deep breath, the warmth of their presence wrapping around me like a cocoon. I felt my heart lifting just a little. We talked about my triggers, the moments of despair that would wash over me like icy waves, and the small victories when I chose to focus on something positive, even if just for a moment.

After our walk, we found a cosy spot with a view of the local pond. We sat on the old cracked wooden bench, the sun warming our faces as I opened up more about my struggles the sleepless nights, the knots in my stomach that showed up unexpectedly, the escape plans during social gatherings, the fear of judgment looming overhead like a storm cloud.

In turn, Dad shared his own challenges how he had not always felt the pressure of being perfect, how he had battled his own demons and could empathize. It was a revelation to learn that my parents had also navigated their own vulnerabilities. They were, after all, human. This shared understanding created a bridge between us that felt like a whisper of hope.

As the afternoon deepened, I realized that talking about my feelings and opening that door was only the beginning. Their willingness to listen gave me the confidence to reclaim my narrative, no longer allowing stigma or shame to define my experience.

Together, we made a pact: to communicate openly, to seek help if needed, and to create a space where it was okay to not be okay. As we strolled back home, the cool breeze danced around us, carrying with it the promise of healing and connection.

That day was not the end; it was just the start of an exploration of understanding and love that I had longed for. The journey might be long and fraught with challenges, but I knew I wouldn't have to face it alone. And for the first time in a while, that felt like enough. As my father and I enjoyed the rugby highlights of this week on TV, my mother spoke to a medical professional to book me an appointment to seek the correct help and support I need.

Good night diary!

Day 2

Dear diary I woke up that morning with a heavy feeling in my chest. It had been weeks since I had a good night's sleep. My mind was constantly racing, replaying every mistake, every failure, every negative thought. I tried to shake it off, but the weight just seemed to get heavier as the day went on. My grades were slipping, my friendships were suffering, and I was constantly on edge. It was the day I had been dreading, but also contemplating for weeks. Today was the appointment with a mental health professional. I had been struggling with self-harm for some time now and I knew it was time to face it head on.

As I sat in the backseat of the car, the weight of the world felt heavier than usual. My parents, concerned yet supportive, exchanged glances in the front as they navigated through traffic. This was more than just a routine visit to the local doctors; it was a pivotal moment in my journey to understand and manage my mental health struggles. The familiar sights of our neighbourhood passed by, but today they felt different tinged with anxiety and hope.

Arriving at the doctor's office, my heart raced. My parents parked the car and I could sense their apprehension, mixed with a determination to help me along this path. They had always been my rock, but this experience was uncharted territory for all of us. As we walked through the waiting room the space that often evokes a mixture of anticipation and anxiety. As you enter, the first thing that captures your attention is the soft, muted lighting, designed to create a calming atmosphere. The walls are adorned with soothing hues of pale blue and gentle greens, while motivational posters and vibrant artwork bring a touch of life to the room. Comfortable chairs, arranged in clusters to promote a sense of community yet providing enough personal space, welcome patients, each one already lost in their thoughts or immersed in a book.

A coffee station occupies one corner, offering a selection of magazines that range from current health topics to the latest fashion trends and items meant to distract and entertain during what can feel like a lengthy wait. The gentle hum of a nearby fish tank adds an element of serenity, the gliding movements of the colourful fish providing a moment of peace amidst the often-stressful experience of visiting a doctor. Meanwhile, the faint sounds of distant voices and medical equipment create an ambient background noise, reminding visitors of the world outside and the purpose of their wait.

In another corner, a children's play area is set up with bright toys and games, a small haven for younger patients. The cheerful chaos of laughter and playful chatter contrasts sharply with the serious nature of the appointment that awaits. As time passes, the rhythmic ticking of the wall clock draws attention to the ticking minutes, building a sense of urgency and impatience.

I could feel the uncomfortable tension in the air, a blend of uncertainty and anticipation. My parents reassured me with soft words and gentle smiles, reminding me that I wasn't alone in this. Sitting in the waiting room of the doctors, a sense of unease mingled with the comforting presence of my parents beside me. The sterile environment was bustling with anxious energy, each person carrying their own burdens and hopes. My parents flanked me, their worried glances darting between the door and the glossy magazines that lay untouched on the table. It was then that I noticed a girl sitting with her parents a few chairs away. She seemed to radiate an unassuming beauty that caught my eye amidst the muted backdrop of the room.

Her hair cascaded in soft waves, a warm chestnut hue that caught the overhead lights and shimmered like gold. With her delicate features adorned by a sprinkling of freckles across her nose, she wore an expression of quiet contemplation as if she were lost in her own thoughts. There was a grace in the way she moved, even in the stillness of her seat, her fingers absentmindedly twisted the bracelet on her wrist, each twist a subtle meditation. She glanced up occasionally, her deep green eyes reflecting a blend of vulnerability and strength that resonated with my own feelings of unease.

What struck me most was the kindness that lingered in her gaze. It felt reassuring, as though she understood the weight of the moment we both found ourselves in. In that fleeting exchange of glances, a connection sparked a silent acknowledgement of our shared experiences. I felt a strange sense of comfort in knowing that I wasn't alone; perhaps she was navigating her own battles, much like I was. The beauty of her presence, combined with the gravity of the situation, made me realise that sometimes, even in places that seem heavy with despair, you can find hints of light and the possibility of understanding among strangers. She fidgeted nervously with her hands. Curiosity sparked within me a silent recognition of our shared experience and a desire to connect.

When we both stood up to get some water at the same time, an unspoken understanding passed between us. As we met at the small water dispenser, I mustered the courage to break the ice.

"Hey my name is Felix, what are you here for?" I asked, my voice barely rising above the soft hum of the fluorescent lights.

Her eyes lit up, revealing a sincerity that instantly put me at ease.

She replied with a calming yet joyful tone. "Hello, my name is Florence but everyone calls me Flo."

We exchanged words briefly, sharing snippets of our lives and the challenges that brought us to this place. It felt oddly comforting to hear someone else articulate feelings I had long struggled to express. In that moment, the world outside our worries faded away, and we found solace in our shared vulnerability a reminder that we were not alone on this journey.

As Flo's name was called out by the doctor passing by, I returned to my respective seats; I felt a flicker of hope and connection. It was heartening to realise that even in the midst of pain, there were others like me grappling with their own mental health challenges. Our brief conversation had transformed a sterile waiting room into a space imbued with empathy and understanding. As I sat down, I caught her eye one last time, and we exchanged a small but genuine smile, silently promising that we would be okay, perhaps even strong enough to help each other navigate the uncertainties that lay ahead. All of a sudden as I saw her being escorted down the long, narrow hall with her parents on either side of her. I knew I had to say something to her or I would spend my day wishing I had because I had never seen such vulnerability with such beauty and grace. So, I peacefully sprinted down the hall, trying so hard not to make a scene. I finally reached her and built up the courage.

"Hello sorry to bother you again, I am not really good at this, but is there any chance we could see each other again, other than in a Doctor's waiting room?" he said in a charming and friendly tone.

She replied in a surprisingly excited tone. "Oh, wow I was not expecting this today, but yeah sure I guess, here is my number and maybe we could get some coffee sometime"

After we exchanged numbers, I slowly made my way back to my parents with mixed feelings inside. I mean, I just asked a girl out. now I have to face my fears and I just reminded myself why I'm here. When my name was called, I took a deep breath and stood up, feeling the gravity of the moment. My parents walked with me to the consultation room, their presence a constant reminder of their love and commitment to my well-being. I knew that this appointment was just the beginning of a long process, but with their support, I felt a flicker of optimism.

As I sat in the doctor's room, my heart was racing. I had never opened up to anyone about my struggles before. But I knew it was necessary if I wanted to get better. I was greeted by a kind-looking man, Dr. Burns. He asked me to tell him a bit about myself and what had brought me here. As I spoke, I could feel the tears welling up in my eyes. It was like a dam had burst and all of my emotions came flooding out. Dr. Burns listened patiently and asked me questions, never judging or interrupting.

"it's ok not to be good all the time. I am here to help, and together, we can get through this difficult time as a united team. How does that sound?" he said in a reassuring voice.

"I know it's hard; I just can't live like this. The voice in my head needs to disappear," I replied.

During our session, he recommended therapy and prescribed me medication to help manage my anxiety and depression. I was hesitant at first, but I knew I needed to give it a try.

I just finished a doctor's appointment with my parents, and it was a significant moment in my journey towards understanding and addressing my mental health struggles. Walking into the clinic, I felt a mix of anxiety and relief. I knew that discussing my self-harming issues would be difficult, but it was also a crucial step toward healing. With my parents by my side, I felt a sense of support, even though the conversation was deeply personal and vulnerable. The doctor listened attentively as I shared my experiences, framing my struggles in a way that helped me feel validated rather than ashamed. The appointment served as a reminder that mental health is an ongoing battle that many faces, yet it's easy to feel isolated in those struggles. My parents asked questions and expressed their concerns, which made me realise that they wanted to understand and help me. It felt empowering to articulate my feelings and explore the reasons behind my actions. We discussed coping strategies, therapies, and the importance of creating a supportive environment at home. At that moment, we walked to the car with a huge understanding of everything. I was especially optimistic about the future ahead; another bonus is I got a date with a stunning girl who also relates to and understands what it's like to feel alone.

As the car hummed softly along the road, a heavy silence settled between us, punctuated only by the occasional rustle of my parents shifting in their seats. We had discussed my mental health struggles openly for the first time, and the vulnerability of sharing my self-harming issues felt raw yet strangely liberating. My parents had listened attentively, their faces a mix of concern and compassion, trying to grasp the depths of my battles while grappling with their own feelings of helplessness.

I stared out the window, watching the scenery of the brick terrace blur by a metaphor for the whirlwind of thoughts racing through my mind. Each passing building felt like a reminder of the distance yet to be traversed, both in healing and understanding. The car's interior was filled with a tense quietude, and I sensed my parents exchanging glances, perhaps worried about how to approach me now or unsure of the right words to offer.

We eventually approached home, my heart raced with mixed emotions: fear of returning to the familiar yet challenging environment and hope for eventual healing. I remembered the doctor's advice about communication and support, reassuring me that I wasn't alone in this struggle. I took a deep breath, feeling the weight of my experiences and the beginning of a new chapter. It was a small step, but facing my mental health head-on felt like the first flicker of light piercing through the fog.

Later on, that evening I had dinner with my parents after a long day at the doctor's was a blend of relief and lingering anxiety. The weight of the day hung heavily in the air, as we gathered around the table, our dining table was my grandparents it served not as a design piece of the home because of the cracking oak wood in its leg, but more of a functional piece, but a reminder I was safe here. The familiar scent of my mother's cooking wrapped around us like a comforting embrace. My mother's cooking was a labour of love, a reminder that amidst the challenges I faced, I had a support system eager to nourish both my body and spirit. As we shared the meal, my parents took turns gently inquiring about my appointment, their concern evident in their eyes.

Conversations flowed from the mundane happenings of their lives to the deeper discussions about my mental health struggles. I felt a mix of vulnerability and safety as I opened up about my feelings, the doctor's words still swirling in my mind. They listened intently, nodding in understanding, devoid of judgment. It was comforting to know that my struggles did not alter their love for me; instead, they reinforced it. With each bite, I felt a gradual easing of my burden, the laughter and warmth of the shared meal providing a balm to my frayed emotions.

Ultimately, that dinner became more than just a meal; it was a reaffirmation of our bond. The evening illuminated the importance of connection, even in the darkest times, as my parents reminded me that it was okay to not be okay. By the time dessert appeared on the table, the heaviness of the day had shifted, at least momentarily. We found peace in each other's presence, reaffirming that love and understanding could be just as nourishing as the food on our plates.

The sun dipped over the terrace houses, leaving a gold ray shining through the windows. I hastily made my way from the kitchen to my room as I was eager to message Flo and ask her how her appointment went. I am, for one, not to get excited this easily, well, I have never asked someone out before, nor have I ever had a girlfriend. However, Tommy has had many girlfriends throughout the years, so I understand how not to be a douchebag. It was about 30 minutes later, and I was staring at my phone like a lost river entering an unknown sea. This was the first time I could not think of what to say or do. Do I say hi, how are you, or should I ask about her appointment and how it went?

All of a sudden, "Buzz Buzz Buzz". My phone had a message, and it was not Tommy. "Hello, I am Florence from the waiting room," it said.

I replied, "Hi, yes, I remember you, how was your day, I bet it was better than mine".

Hours slipped by unnoticed as our conversation deepened, transcending the mundane worries that initially surrounded us. We discovered shared interests, from favourite movies to obscure hobbies, and each topic seemed to ignite newfound excitement. Did you know she also likes vintage clothing and reading fantasy novels? I could not have pictured my day ending like this.

That night, as the darkness settled outside, our phones buzzed with messages. What began as light-hearted banter quickly evolved into a night-long dialogue filled with dream-sharing, personal anecdotes, and dreams of the future. Each notification brought a rush of anticipation, and I found myself captivated by her thoughts and insights. As hours passed, the once-strange familiarity transformed into a comforting companionship that extended beyond our brief meeting. Who would have thought that a simple wait at the doctor's office could lead to an unforgettable night spent connecting with someone so intriguing? For the first time in years, I did not worry about my mental health or wonder what I might do to myself, it was like my mind was in a blockhouse.

"I should really get to bed because It's been a long day," I said.

"ok, no problem, let's talk again soon." She replied.

Good night diary!

Day 5

Dear diary I don't even know where to start. I guess I should start with the doctor's appointment I had a few days ago. Honestly, it was a bit like stepping into a ring with my own mind, a wrestling match where I was the unwilling participant. As soon as I walked into that small room, I felt the air shift. The doctor was kind, but he had this way of getting right to the heart of things like an arrow hitting the bullseye without hesitation.

He asked about my struggles with anxiety and the moments when the world seemed too big, and too demanding. There was this part of me that wanted to say it wasn't a big deal, that I could handle it all on my own, but the truth is it has been weighing me down like a heavy stone. Talking about it was like letting out a breath I didn't know I was holding in.

He gave me some strategies for breathing exercises, and journaling (hello, this diary!), and even encouraged me to reach out to friends more often. But one thing he said stuck with me: "You're not alone in this." Those five words cut through the fog of loneliness I often felt, reminding me that everyone has their own battles.

Since that appointment, I've been trying to put his advice into practice. I signed up for a local book club, something I never thought I'd do. The thought of it made me nervous, but I figured if I was going to face my fears, I might as well do it head-on. And who knows? Maybe I'll find a little peace. Once at the I arrived at the local library where the club was being held, after my dad dropped me off I nervously walked inside.

Then there's her. I can't believe how nervous I get just thinking about texting her. I met Florence in the waiting of the doctor's and we talked all night. Now we are at the same club. when I was drowning in my thoughts, trying to find some clarity, I built up the courage and nervously went over and talked to her.

"Hi, it's me, Felix, remember me from yesterday," I said

"Are you joining the book club as well"? she replied with an energetic tone.

"I was thinking about it, the doctor said I need to get out more to take my mind off everything".

We ended up chatting the whole session, and it felt oddly natural like we'd known each other for ages, rather than just a few minutes. There was a glow about her, the way she laughed that seemed to light up the dim corners of my mind.

We started texting only 1 day ago, and it's been both exhilarating and terrifying. I find myself grappling with the urge to overthink every message, worried I might say something stupid. But when she replies, it feels like each buzz from my phone is a little spark of hope. Today, she mentioned her love for hiking, and I couldn't help but feel a rush of excitement at the prospect of maybe joining her someday. Well, I have not hiked before, but it's just walking, right?

What if I mess it up? What if she's not interested? But then that familiar voice inside me chimes in, reminding me of the doctor's words. Take a step forward. Life doesn't wait for perfection.

Later on, after the session we both went our separate ways. So, I asked, tentatively suggesting we meet up for coffee, real coffee this time, not just the virtual kind through a screen. My heart raced as I hit send, and I stood up from my desk and paced my room, waiting for her response.

A few minutes later, my phone buzzed. It felt like a small eternity, but there it was.

"Coffee sounds great! Let's do it!"

And just like that, a sliver of light pierced through the smog of my worries. For the first time in a while, I felt a flicker of excitement. Perhaps I can learn to juggle both: my mental health struggles and opening up to someone who, for some reason, seems to get me.

It was one of those serendipitous evenings, where the stars seemed to align just right. I spent the entire night engrossed in a conversation with a girl I had only met a few days ago. As the glow of my phone lit up the dark room, each notification felt like a lifeline. Our exchange flowed effortlessly, filled with laughter, shared interests, and deeper thoughts that stretched far beyond surface-level small talk. In a world that often feels isolating, those hours felt like a refuge. In her words, I found solace a temporary escape from the swirling thoughts that plagued me, the anxiety that often kept me awake at night.

But as moon approached, reality began to seep back in. Despite the comfort of our connection, I couldn't shake the weight of my own mental health struggles. Conversations like ours offered a brief reprieve, but I was all too aware of the underlying battles I faced daily. I tried to balance the joy of discovering someone new with the shadows of my own mind, wondering if I could truly engage in something real while feeling so fractured inside. Still, something was comforting in the way she listened, the way she shared her own vulnerabilities. Each shared detail felt like a small step toward healing, both for her and for me, even if the journey was just beginning. As the sun began to rise, casting a golden hue over everything, I realized that maybe, just maybe, this new connection could serve as a guiding light through my struggles. We ended our long yet wonderful evening by deciding to meet up for coffee at the local village coffee shop the next day. This was a big step mentally; however, I knew it was right.

Good night diary!

Day 6

Dear diary the morning of my first date dawned bright and early, sunlight filtering through the curtains, casting a warm glow across my room. As I blinked awake, excitement mingled with a sense of dread, my heart racing at the prospect of meeting someone new. Yet, beneath the thrill lurked the familiar shadows of my mental health struggles. Anxiety wrapped its tendrils around my thoughts, whispering doubts and insecurities that threatened to overshadow the day's potential. I ran through my checklist in my mind: what to wear, what to say, and how to ensure that I didn't let my worries ruin this special moment.

I moved through my morning routine like a robot, brushing my teeth, showering, and picking out an outfit, all while a whirlwind of emotions swirled within me. Moments of hope contrasted sharply with feelings of inadequacy, heavily weighing down my spirit. Would I be able to keep the conversation flowing? Would my nervous tendencies be too apparent? I found myself wrestling with the impulse to retreat into my comfort zone, yet there was a flicker of determination in my chest. Perhaps this date could be a step toward healing, a chance to connect with someone who might understand my battles.

As I stood in front of the mirror, I took a deep breath, trying to summon a sense of calm. I reminded myself that it was okay to be vulnerable and that sharing my experiences might even build a bridge of understanding with my date. With my heart pounding and a practised smile on my face, I stepped out the door, ready to embrace whatever the day had in store, one cautious foot in front of the other.

I pushed the door, a small bell jingling above him as he stepped into the warm embrace of the coffee shop. The familiar rich aroma of roasted beans wrapped around him like a comforting blanket, but today, it felt a bit heavier. He wiped his palms against his jeans, looking around for the one he had only met through the glowing screen of his phone.

After exchanging texts for nearly a week, he finally gathered the courage to suggest a meetup. They had laughed about it during their late-night conversations, and he could sense a connection forming between them, but now that he was here, the weight of anxiety settled in his chest like a stone.

My phone buzzed in my pocket, and he fished it out hesitantly. A message flashed on the screen:

"I'm here! Can't wait to finally meet in person again!"

It was from Flo, the girl whose laughter had charmed him through text messages, exposing a side of her that felt both relatable and distant.

I scanned the room in search of her, catching sight of a girl in the corner, her chestnut hair spilling over her shoulders as she peered down at her phone with a smile. There she is. I mustered his courage and walked toward her, his heart racing.

"Hey, Flo?" he said, his voice slightly shaky.

She looked up, her eyes bright with recognition. "Felix! Wow, it's so good to finally meet you other than a library or a waiting room!" She stood up and hugged him tightly, and for a moment, the world around him faded away.

"Yeah, you too," I replied, releasing her as a warm blush tinted his cheeks. We both settled into our seats with delicious drinks in hand. I couldn't help but notice the way she tapped her fingers nervously against the table, and he wondered if she felt the same jitters he did or if she was going through similar situations.

As we sipped our drinks, we began to share stories, the conversation flowing as easily as the gentle hum of chatter around them. Flo told me about her love for photography and the way she captured moments that seemed too precious to forget. I shared my passion for music, revealing how I poured my emotions into lyrics to cope with the chaos in his mind. With every story they exchanged, the gaps filled in like pieces of a jigsaw puzzle.

"Do you ever feel like everything is just... too much?" Flo asked, her gaze dropping to her coffee cup.

I caught the flicker of vulnerability in her eyes. I knew that familiar feeling all too well the overwhelming weight of expectations, the swirling storm of thoughts that would sometimes drown him.

"Definitely. Some days, it feels like I'm just treading water and others, I can barely keep my head above the surface," he confessed, his voice barely above a whisper.

Flo looked up, her expression softening. "I feel the same way. It's tough to talk about, especially with people who don't understand."

"I get that," Felix replied, feeling a connection deepen between them. "But I'm glad we found each other. It sometimes helps just knowing someone gets it."

They fell into a comfortable silence, sipping their juices as they allowed the moment to linger. It felt refreshing to share their struggles with someone who didn't shy away from vulnerability. In that little coffee shop, behind the walls of their mental health battles, they began building a space that felt safe and familiar.

Just before the afternoon sun began to dip below the horizon, Flo said, "You know, I had my doubts about meeting up. I was afraid it wouldn't live up to the conversation we had over text."

I smiled, a sense of relief washing over him. "Same here. But this… this has been really nice."

Unexpectedly, a laugh bubbled from Flo, bright and infectious, quelling the remnants of his earlier anxiety. It reminded him of the way her texts sparkled with optimism even amidst the seriousness they often discussed.

As we prepared to leave, Flo hesitated. "Hey, I don't want this to just be a one-time thing. Can we keep talking? Maybe grab drinks again sometime?"

my heart skipped at her words. "I'd really like that."

With a promise to meet again soon, we stepped back into the world outside, brewed awakening, where the sky was now painted in hues of pink and gold. For the first time in a long while, I felt a flicker of hope ignite within him that maybe, just maybe, I had found not only a friend but also a partner to navigate the complexities of life together.

It was one of those serendipitous evenings, where the stars seemed to align just right. I spent the entire night engrossed in a conversation with Flo, whom I had only met a few days ago. As the glow of my phone lit up the dark room, each notification felt like a lifeline. Our exchange flowed effortlessly, filled with laughter, shared interests, and deeper thoughts that stretched far beyond surface-level small talk. In a world that often feels isolating, those hours felt like a refuge. In her words, I found solace a temporary escape from the swirling thoughts that plagued me, the anxiety that often kept me awake at night.

But as dawn approached, reality began to seep back in. Despite the comfort of our connection, I couldn't shake the weight of my own mental health struggles. Conversations like ours offered a brief reprieve, but I was all too aware of the underlying battles I faced daily. I tried to balance the joy of discovering someone new with the shadows of my own mind, wondering if I could truly engage in something real while feeling so fractured inside. Still, something was comforting in the way she listened, the way she shared her own vulnerabilities. Each shared detail felt like a small step toward healing, both for her and for me, even if the journey was just beginning, I realized that maybe, just maybe, this new connection could serve as a guiding light through my struggles.

Good night diary!

Day 7

Dear diary the morning sun streamed through the curtains, casting soft shadows across the room. I woke up, my heart racing a familiar, unwelcome guest. Today was my first day of therapy, a step I'd been avoiding for far too long, yet somehow it felt like a last resort. I had spent countless nights wrestling with my thoughts, each one more chaotic than the last, and now, I found myself at a fork in the road, clutching onto the hope that maybe this path would lead me to some semblance of peace.

In the bathroom mirror, I stared at my reflection, taking in the dark circles under my eyes a testament to the sleepless nights and the weight of the world I had been carrying. I splashed cold water on my face, threw on a pair of jeans, and chose a hoodie that felt like a shield against the world. I wasn't ready to bare my soul just yet; I needed my armour.

Later on, that morning arriving at the therapist's office, I felt a wave of anxiety wash over me. The brick building loomed like a fortress of unfamiliarity, but I took a deep breath and stepped inside. The waiting area was warm and inviting, decorated with soft colours and an array of plants that seemed to breathe life into the sterile environment. I clutched the strap of my bag tightly, scanning the room for familiar faces, but I was alone, and the solitude amplified my anxiety.

I landed myself in a plush chair, trying to focus on a coffee table with books about landscapes, but my mind was too loud. Flashbacks of my struggles swirled in an unending loop the times I had felt invisible, the moments I had convinced myself that I was a burden, the laughter that had turned into tears. I pulled my knees to my chest, feeling small and vulnerable.

After what felt like an eternity, a woman entered the room, her warm smile breaking through the cloud of my apprehension. "Hi! I'm Dr. Brittan," she said, her voice soothing like a soft melody. "You must be here for our session."

I nodded, managing to muster a quiet, "Yeah." For the first time in a long while, I felt seen, and it frightened me.

As I followed her into the therapy room basing busy corridors filled with multiple photos of colours and serene landscapes, I was hit with a wave of emotion a blend of anticipation and dread. The room was furnished with comfortable chairs and calming art on the walls, designed for safety. I sat down, forcing myself to unlock my grip on the bag which contained my carefully curated façade. I had spent so long concealing the darkness that had seeped into my life, the shame and fear cloaked in a smile.

"Tell me about what brought you here," Dr. Brittan encouraged gently, her eyes patient and understanding.

I hesitated, words dancing on the tip of my tongue but refusing to step forward. So, I spoke about the generalities the stress from all the bullying, and the strain in my relationship with my friend easily glossing over the depth of my struggles. I was so practised at concealing the truth that I could construct a narrative without revealing its raw edges.

She listened, nodding, but I could see the quiet question in her eyes. She challenged me, not with pressure but with gentle nudges. "And how does that make you feel?"

The question hung in the air, vast and disorienting. I paused, my façade beginning to crack, memories surfacing that I had buried deep. "I don't know if I can…," I stammered, my voice wavering. It felt like standing on a precipice, terrified to look down.

"You're in a safe space," she assured me. "It's okay to feel."

Her reassurance slowly began to peel away layers of my carefully constructed shield. I started to talk about the voice in my head, the one that pushed me to the brink, the one that whispered lies about my worth. Each word felt like a weight lifted, a release I hadn't anticipated.

I spoke of the moment during a crowded event when I felt so profoundly alone, surrounded by laughter that felt foreign to me. How I had smiled and engaged, all while drowning inside. I told her about the times I wanted to scream to the world that I was hurting, yet instead, I opted to play the role of the clown, masking my pain with humor, concealing my vulnerability.

With each admission, I felt lighter, like I was slowly revealing a hidden garden amidst a forest of shadows. Dr. Brittan listened intently, guiding me with probing questions, gently encouraging me to dig deeper into my emotional landscape.

As the session ended, I was surprised by how the heaviness in my chest had started to dissipate. It was only the beginning, a single step on a winding road, but it felt monumental. I realized I wouldn't be able to conceal the depths of my struggles anymore, but maybe, just maybe, I could learn to embrace them.

Walking back to my car park where my parents were waiting for me, I felt the weight of the world still resting on my shoulders, but it was a little lighter. I had started to peel back the layers, exposing raw, beautiful truth to the light, and for the first time, I felt the promise of healing whisper in my ear. It wasn't just about concealing the pain; it was about allowing myself to feel it and, ultimately, to heal.

As I settled into the backseat of the car after my therapy appointment, a familiar blend of exhaustion and relief washed over me. The soft hum of the engine provided a comforting backdrop as my parents chatted quietly in the front seat, their voices a gentle reminder that I wasn't alone in this journey. The session had been intense, filled with emotions I often kept bottled up. I reflected on the vulnerability I felt while discussing my mental health struggles, a mix of anxiety and frustration that seemed to creep in and out of my life. The words of my therapist echoed in my mind, encouraging me to embrace my feelings rather than shy away from them.

As we drove through familiar streets, I found myself staring out the window, watching the world rush by. Each passing dog walker and storefront felt like a reminder of the challenges I faced daily moments of overwhelming sadness, thoughts that spiralled without warning, and the constant search for light amid the darkness. I felt a pang of gratitude for my parents, who were my unwavering support system, always willing to listen and learn about what I was experiencing. I could sense their concern, but also their determination to understand and help me navigate these turbulent waters.

The conversation eventually shifted as my mom asked how I felt about today's session. I took a deep breath, gathering my thoughts before sharing some insights about my therapy journey. It was comforting to articulate my struggles in a space free of judgment, and I appreciated how my parents actively engaged in the discussion, making it clear that they wanted to be part of my healing process. The ride home was bittersweet while I grappled with the weight of my mental health challenges. It was a nuanced balance of fear and optimism, reminding me that although the road ahead may be bumpy, I was not travelling it alone.

That night was one of those moments that felt both heavy and cathartic, as I found myself deep in conversation with Flo, trading texts under the gentle glow of my bedside lamp. We had lost track of time, ensconced in our own little world, where distance and sleepiness faded away, leaving only the raw honesty of our exchange. I shared with her the details of my therapy session earlier that day, a mix of vulnerability and relief washing over me as I articulated my mental health struggles. It's not always easy to put into words the spirals of anxiety and bouts of sadness that cloud my mind, but with her, it felt safe; she listened without judgment, offering insights and reassurance that eased the weight on my heart.

As I typed out my feelings, I could sense her support wrapped around me like a warm blanket, as if she were right there beside me. Her texts offered validation, affirming that my struggles were valid and that I wasn't alone in this battle. Talking about my therapy sessions allowed us to peel back layers, revealing not just the challenges I faced but also the small victories I cherished. With each message, I felt the burden lighten, the connection between us growing stronger. It was a powerful reminder that mental health discussions are not just about pain; they are also about healing, love, and resilience, allowing both of us to understand each other struggles better. It was a night filled with emotion, yet comforting a gentle beacon of hope amidst the darkness I often navigate.

Good night diary!

Day 8

Dear diary yesterday was a day woven from simple threads, a tapestry hung within the walls of our cosy home. The sun filtered softly through the curtains, casting warm patches of light that danced across the hardwood floors. I awoke with a lingering heaviness that came after sharing an intimate piece of myself, a sensation that draped itself over my shoulders like a familiar blanket. The day before had been filled with words my struggles with anxiety, the shadows of depression shared in the safe space of a therapist's office. Now, however, it was time to step into the comforting embrace of my family.

I shuffled my way to the kitchen, the aroma of freshly brewed coffee swirling into my senses. There was my mom, standing by the stove, her long hair pulled into a loose bun, wearing the same oversized sweater she loved for its warmth. She turned to me, her face lighting up with a gentle smile, one that whispered of unconditional support. Dad was reading the newspaper at the table, his brow furrowed in concentration. He looked up, catching my eye, and offered a nod of understanding.

"Good morning, sleepyhead," Mom said, her voice warm and inviting. "How did you sleep?"

"Okay, I guess," I replied, rubbing the remnants of sleep from my eyes. "Just... thinking."

"That's alright," Dad chimed in, folding the newspaper. "We're here for anything you need, no pressure."

I slid into a chair at the table, finding comfort in the familiarity of our morning routine. The day stretched ahead, a canvas of possibilities, but I knew that some quiet time was essential for me, especially today. I needed to breathe, to allow the echoes of yesterday to settle and morph into something less daunting.

After breakfast, I retreated to my sanctuary my bedroom. The walls, painted in soft, muted hues, felt like a safe cocoon. I wandered to the shelf lined with books, each one a portal to another world. I picked up a novel, one I had meant to read ages ago, its cover dog-eared and faded from previous visits. With a comfortable nest of blankets surrounding me, I settled on my bed and opened the pages.

As I delved into the story, I lost myself in the words. Each character's journey reminded me that struggles, no matter how solitary they feel, are part of the broader tapestry of life. The soothing rhythm of the words blended seamlessly with the soft melodies streaming from my speakers. Music enveloped me like a hug, its notes wrapping around my heart, guiding my thoughts into a space of reflection and calm.

Hours melted away as I read and listened, the world outside my window vibrating softly with life yet feeling distant. My mom occasionally peeked in, her presence a gentle reminder that I was not alone in my solitude. She would check if I needed anything, her cuts of concern blending seamlessly with easy laughter when I would chuckle at a particularly funny line from my book.

Eventually, my dad knocked and entered, suggesting a game of cards.

"You want to take a break from all that reading? Come on, I'll let you win today," he joked, waggling his eyebrows playfully.

I couldn't help but smile it was a light-hearted challenge, the kind that made our afternoons memorable.

We gathered in the living room, the coffee table adorned with a deck of cards and a bowl of popcorn. Mom joined us, her laughter filling the room like music. The game was filled with playful banter, strategic card plays, and the occasional disagreement over rules that would inevitably dissolve into fits of laughter. It felt good, this simple ritual shared with my parents a mix of competition and camaraderie that reminded me of home.

The world outside continued spinning, but at this moment, everything felt serene. I found myself slipping away from my worries, laughter breaking the surface tension of lingering anxiety.

By the time the sun began to dip below the horizon, painting the sky with shades of gold and purples, I felt lighter. We had shared a day of connection, a blanket of support covering my heart as I navigated the chaos of my mind. Though the struggles of yesterday remained, today was a gentle reminder that I didn't have to face them alone.

As I climbed into bed later that night, the weight on my chest wasn't gone, but it was softer and more bearable. As I closed my eyes, I realized that sometimes, all it took was a day spent with family, wrapped in laughter and love, to offer a little solace.

Good night diary!

Day 9

Dear diary the sun had barely risen above the rooftops, casting a warm, golden light into my small apartment. I stood in front of the mirror, my hands trembling slightly as I tucked in the patterned sweater vest I got for my birthday a few years ago. This was the morning of my second coffee date with Flo, a girl whose laughter lingered in my mind long after our first meeting. Our last encounter had felt like a fleeting moment of connection in a world that often felt heavy.

I indulged in a moment of reflection, letting my mind wander to the first date. We had met at a quaint little local café nestled on a bustling street corner of the village. It had been a little chaotic, with a local artist's market happening outside. The memory of her smile, bright and genuine, made my heart flutter in a way I hadn't felt in a long time. But underneath all the excitement, a familiar weight settled into my chest. My mental health had been a constant battle, an unwelcome companion that often clouded my thoughts and drained my energy.

"Just breathe," I whispered to myself, trying to dispel the anxiety that crept up as I thought about today's date. It was easy to focus on the positives Flo was kind-hearted and easy to talk to; she had shown genuine interest in my passions. But the darker parts of my mind kept whispering harmfully What if you don't make her laugh this time? What if she sees how heavy you really are?

With a sigh, I poured myself a cup of coffee, letting the familiar aroma envelop me like a warm hug. I hoped it would provide me with the jolt I needed to push through my unease. I took a deep breath, inhaling the rich scent, reminding myself that this was a chance to connect, share, and maybe even heal a little in the company of someone who made me feel seen.

As I stepped outside, the crisp morning air greeted me with a cool kiss. I took a moment to admire the vibrant flowers lining the sidewalks, their colours cheerful against the brick buildings. I walked to the café, determined to keep my head up. The gentle hum of conversation surrounded us as I entered into the cosy café, the aroma of freshly brewed coffee permeating the air. It was our second date, and I could feel the familiar mix of excitement and anxiety churning in my stomach.

Her name was Florence, but everyone calls her Flo, and we had met a few days ago earlier in a waiting room of a doctor's clinic. Our first date had been filled with laughter, casual conversation, and an easy connection that felt both exhilarating and terrifying. But now, with the anticipation of this second meeting, the shadows of my mental health issues crept back in those whispers of self-doubt and anxiety that always seemed to surface when I wanted things to go well.

I watched as Flo entered the café, her presence illuminating the space. Her hair danced lightly in the breeze as she brushed it back, the sunlight highlighting her warm smile. I waved, and she approached with a smile that made my heart race. There was something magnetic about her, something that pulled me closer, yet my mind wrestled with its own chaos.

"Hey! Sorry I'm a bit late," she said, sliding into the chair across from me. "I got caught up trying to decide what to wear."

"No worries," I replied, forcing a smile to mask the tumult inside. "You look great."

Flo's cheeks flushed a light pink, and she looked down at the table, clearly pleased. The conversation flowed easily at first talking about our favourite books, music, and the oddities of life in the city. But every so often, a flicker of anxiety would stab at me, reminding me that with every shared laugh, there was an unspoken fear lurking beneath the surface.

The barista an older man with a scruffy beard and kind eyes brought over our drinks, a cosy strawberry punch for Flo and a pineapple juice for me. I took a moment to appreciate the rich aroma, hoping to ground myself in the present, but my mind raced ahead. Would she still like me if she knew about my struggles? Would she think I was too broken, too complicated?

"So, what do you do when you're not enjoying a delightful coffee date?" Flo asked, her animated eyes inviting me to share more.

I hesitated, searching for the right words. My instinct was to keep the darker parts of my life hidden, but there was a genuine curiosity in her gaze that made me consider being honest. "Well, I, but I also… I struggle with anxiety and depression," I confessed, my heart pounding as the words left my lips.

Flo's expression softened. "Thank you for sharing that with me. I can't imagine it's easy," she said, sincerity lacing her voice.

A wave of emotion washed over me, a mixture of relief and vulnerability. "It's not always easy. Some days are better than others. But I'm working on it."

"Good for you," she replied, her voice steady. "It takes courage to share that. I have my own battles too, you know. It helps to talk about them."

I felt a connection deepen between us, the walls I had constructed beginning to crumble. She shared her own struggles with self-acceptance, her tendency to overthink situations, and how sometimes, her own mind felt like a maze she couldn't escape.

At that moment, the café buzzed around us, but it felt like we were wrapped in our own little world. Our vulnerabilities created a tapestry of understanding, a shared fragility that brought us closer together.

As we finished our drinks, I realized that the date hadn't only been about impressing her or maintaining an ideal facade. It was about connection, honesty, and the courage to be ourselves, imperfections and all.

"Would you like to go for a walk?" I asked, feeling a spark of hope flicker within me.

Flo's eyes brightened. "I'd love that."

The warm glow of the café lingered as we stepped out into the crisp spring air, a slight chill brushing over our skin. The leaves crunched beneath our feet as we walked side by side, a pleasant silence filling the spaces between us. Flo had a way of making the world feel lighter; her laughter was like sunlight breaking through the clouds, illuminating the heavy shadows that so often clouded my mind.

It had taken a deep breath and a leap of faith to share my mental health struggles with her. I had wrestled with the decision, unsure if my honesty would push her away or bring us closer. But as she listened, her eyes filled with understanding rather than judgment, I found comfort in her presence. She reminded me that vulnerability doesn't equal weakness.

I glanced sideways at her, catching a glimpse of her smile framed by auburn hair that danced in the gentle wind. Her cheeks were adorned with a soft blush, probably from the cold, but it only heightened her allure. I couldn't help but feel a fluttering sensation in my stomach the kind that sparks hope, excitement, and a hint of fear. What if this moment was the beginning of something beautiful?

We strolled past the quaint brick houses in the village, their windows glowing like warm eyes watching over us. I pointed out a particularly charming house, boasting a garden that looked like a painter's palette, filled with vibrant hues of marigold and crimson.

"I could see myself settling down in a place like that," I mused, and to my surprise, she turned to me, her gaze steady.

"Do you dream of a life in the village?" she asked, curiosity dancing in her voice.

"Sometimes," I replied, my mind flickering through images of a quiet life gardening on Sundays, morning coffees on the porch, and laughter echoing within the walls. But it felt surreal to share such thoughts with someone I had just met. "I guess I'm just searching for some peace," I added, feeling a mix of vulnerability and strength in my honesty.

She nodded, her expression thoughtful. "We all are, in one way or another," she said, almost as if she had stood in my shoes before. "But I believe that's the essence of living. It's in the struggle that we find our way."

As we continued our walk, I felt an invisible thread weaving between us, binding our stories hers of childhood dreams and mine of battles fought in the quiet of my mind. Each step-built confidence, reassuring me that perhaps revealing my heart wasn't a mistake after all.

We reached the edge of a small pond, the surface reflecting the vibrant sky above. An old wooden bench sat nearby, and we took a moment to pause. Flo sat first, and I followed, finding solace in the familiar warmth of conversation. We laughed, shared memories of our favourite books, and discovered a shared love for the ocean's rhythm and the magic of twilight.

"I've always thought the sea has a way of healing," she said softly, her gaze resting on the pond. "It's like it understands our struggles, washing away stress with every wave."

"Yes! Just being near it calms me down." I could sense the openness in our dialogue like the layers of our hearts were gradually unravelling. "I used to walk along the beach whenever I felt overwhelmed. The sound of the waves crashing made me feel less alone."

"What about now?" she asked, tilting her head as she studied me. "What do you do when it gets tough?"

I hesitated for a moment, contemplating how much to unfold. Eventually, I decided to paint a more vulnerable portrait. "Sometimes I write. Pouring my thoughts on paper helps me understand what I'm feeling. It's like talking to a friend without the fear of judgment."

Florence smiled gently, and the way she looked at me ignited a warmth that spread through my chest. "I'd love to read your writing someday. It sounds beautiful, just like you're letting it be."

In that moment, something shifted. The air around us thickened with unspoken words, tantalizing but somehow intimate. I realized I didn't just fancy her; there was something deeper blooming within me, a tender connection based on authenticity.

As we sat side by side, a soft breeze rippling through the trees, I felt the distance between us shrink. Those shared moments of vulnerability and laughter wrapped us in a cocoon of trust. I turned to her, wanting to seize the moment, hoping to express everything bottled inside.

"Flo," I began, a flutter of nerves tugging at my heart. "I know this might be sudden, but I think I'm starting to fall for you."

She blinked, and for a second, anxiety washed over me, worried I had jeopardized our budding friendship. But then, a radiant smile spread across her face, illuminating the dimming afternoon.

"You're not alone," she replied softly. "I feel it too."

In that tranquil setting, with the world fading away, I took her hand in mine. The warmth of her touch melted away the last remnants of doubt. As the sun dipped below the horizon, painting the sky with hues of orange and pink, I realized that perhaps love wasn't just a feeling; it was a journey we would embark on together, one filled with understanding, acceptance, and the promise of hope.

So, at that moment, I sensed a gut feeling that I should kiss her while we were both vulnerable. Leaned over, grabbed her by the hand, pulled her in, and kissed her softly on the lips. It felt wonderful, and nerve-racking, but most of all it felt right.

In a split second, I pulled away and said "Sorry... I did not mean..., I mean was that ok."

"that was... wow... perfect" she replied pulling me right back in to kiss again.

We both had never felt so safe in one another before; it was like someone had put a protective force field around us.

The weight of my thoughts lifted as I felt the warmth of her lips against mine, a tangible reminder of the beauty found in human connection. It's funny how a simple act like a kiss can evoke such a flurry of emotions, bringing both comfort and vulnerability. As I walked Florence home I held her hand, hoping to hold onto that feeling, knowing that navigating my mental health challenges would always be part of my journey. Yet with her beside me, I realized that perhaps I didn't have to bear that weight alone. Each step toward her house was a blend of anticipation and hope, a feeling that perhaps in this world of chaos, love could be a guiding light, helping me to find balance amid the storm of my thoughts.

As we reached her house I let go of her soft warm hand and told her "I had a wonderful day, I never felt like this before in my whole life."

"I had the best time today, see you soon, Felix Jones", she replied in a funny yet loving tone.

Flo waved goodbye as she closed her front door and at that time all I wanted to do was run home and write about my day in my diary, so I did just that.

Good night diary!

Day 10

Dear diary the first morning after our second date was filled with a mix of excitement and nervousness. I woke up, replaying the moments of our first kiss in my head, my heart still fluttering from the joy of it all. As I made my way downstairs, a smile lingered on my face. The aroma of breakfast wafted through the house, a comforting reminder of the warmth my family always provided. Seated at the table, I nervously decided it was time to share the news about the girl called Florence I'd been seeing.

"Mum, Dad can I tell you something," I told them excitedly

"yes of, course what the matter" my mother replied nervously because the last time I spoke to them like this was when I was at my worst.

I said, "I've been seeing this girl, Florence, she has also had hard times, but she is beautiful, we have lots in common and before you ask Mum we have only kissed".

My parents listened intently, their eyes lighting up with genuine happiness. Their support meant the world to me, especially as I navigate my own struggles with mental health.

Opening up about her felt like a step toward brighter days. At that moment, I realized how powerful it can be to share your heart with those you trust. My parents' joy was infectious, and as they asked me questions about her, I felt a sense of relief wash over me. Despite the challenges I face mentally, this new chapter in my life brought a flicker of hope—a reminder that connections can heal and uplift the spirit. It was a beautiful start to the day, and as I enjoyed breakfast with my family, I felt a growing sense of optimism about what was to come.

After my breakfast, I slipped into my favourite blue sweater vest, feeling its familiar fabric hug my frame. It was a chilly morning, and the warmth of the vest provided a sense of comfort as I stepped outside. I decided to take a walk, yearning for space to breathe and a moment alone with my thoughts my mother yelled "Can you stop by the local shop and get some more milk please" as was walking out the front door. As I made my way down the street, I noticed my neighbours buzzing with excitement; they were having a new kitchen-built start today. The sound of hammers and laughter filled the air, a stark contrast to the stillness I sought. The postman ambled by, delivering letters and packages, his presence a reminder of the everyday life that continued around me, even as I wrestled with my own internal battles.

Turning toward the local pond, I felt the tension in my mind begin to ease with each step. The sun peeked through the trees, casting dappled golden light on the water's surface, and the gentle breeze carried the sweet fragrance of blooming flowers. This spring weather felt revitalizing, a welcome embrace after the long winter. As I strolled along the path, I watched the ducks glide serenely across the pond, their calm demeanour contrasting sharply with the turmoil I sometimes felt within. It struck me how nature could offer peace even when my mental health felt like a turbulent sea. Lost in this quiet moment, I realized that despite the weight of my struggles, brief escapes like these were essential for finding clarity and peace, even if just for a little while.

Following my walk around the local pond, the cool breeze intertwined with the warmth of the sun, bringing a fleeting sense of tranquillity. The rhythmic sound of water lapping against the shore and the distant chorus of birds provided a soothing backdrop to my thoughts. However, as I strolled, the weight of my mental health struggles lingered in the back of my mind. My mother's voice echoed in my ears, reminding me to stop by the local shop to pick up some milk. It was a simple task, yet in my current state, even the smallest errands felt overwhelming.

As I approached the shop, the familiar sight of its bright signage brought a sense of comfort, yet anxiety simmered beneath the surface. This local shop has been in the village for as long as I can remember. The gentle chime of the doorbell as I entered signified a shift from the solitude of nature to the busyness of everyday life. I navigated the aisles, my heart racing slightly at the thought of running into someone I knew. Picking up the milk felt mundane, but in that moment, it represented a small victory a connection to normalcy amidst a turbulent inner landscape.

Suddenly I headed home. The sun was just beginning to set, casting a warm glow on the streets I had walked down countless times. The rhythmic crunch of leaves underfoot accompanied me on my journey, a comforting reminder of the season's beauty.

Upon arriving home, I placed the milk on the kitchen counter and greeted my mum with a bright smile. Her eyes lit up with gratitude as she thanked me, and I felt a small swell of pride for being able to help her with such a simple task. Once my chores were complete, I retreated to my room, eager to escape into the world of the fantasy book I had recently started.

As I settled into my favourite chair, the pages cracked open with promise. The story whisked me away to distant lands filled with magic, adventure, and characters that felt as real as my own family. I lost track of time, immersing myself in the unfolding plot, each turn of the page igniting my imagination. that moment, I was lost in the pages of my fantasy book, enveloped in a world far removed from my own, where dragons soared and heroes embarked on epic quests. Yet, I couldn't shake the feeling of anticipation that pulsed through me as I glanced at my phone, which suddenly lit up with a text. It was from Flo who I had fallen for after just two enchanting dates. We had shared laughter and stories, and our conversations had ventured into deeper territory, including my mental health struggles. As I read her message, a simple inquiry about my day, a rush of warmth spread through me, juxtaposed against the shadowy corners of my mind where anxiety and self-doubt lurked.

"Hi Felix Jones, how was your day, I bet it was better than mine." She texted.

'my day was ok, I guess... wait what happened" I replied promptly.

"well our family cat just died, well she was really old and we all knew it was going to happen soon anyway. I just did anticipate how hard it would be" she said.

"I am so sorry for your loss. It sounds like she had a happy and long life, but you will get through this. If I was with you now I would give you a big hug to let you know that you have my support." I replied.

"That is so sweet, I know it will be hard but maybe later on this week we could go to the cinema together, so I can lose my mind in a film." She said.

"yes, that would be wonderful, I am looking forward to it. However, it's getting late, so good night Flo" I responded.

"Good night Felix Jones" she returned

The excitement, because she had become a brighter spot in my life, a person who seemed to genuinely care. Her kindness cut through the haze of my struggles, reminding me that even in darkness, there were glimmers of connection and hope. It was a delicate balance to maintain; the joy of her presence fighting against the weight of my own challenges.

Good night, diary!

Day 11

Dear diary the morning sunlight streamed through my window, casting a warm glow over my room as I woke up. It was the day of my second therapy session, and the mixed feelings churned in my stomach like a blender that refused to turn off. I swung my legs over the side of the bed and sat momentarily, rubbing the sleep from my eyes. Memories of last night floated back: countless messages exchanged with Flo, her laughter echoing in my mind. Talking to her felt so easy, so natural like breathing.

I quickly threw on an old sweater vest onto of a t shirt and jeans, simple staples that never asked for much. In the kitchen, my parents were already up. The smell of toast filled the air, mingling with the faint scent of coffee. My mother buzzed around, making sure everything was perfect, and my father sat at the table flipping through the newspaper. I sensed the concern in their eyes, the unspoken worry about my mental health. It hovered in the room like a cloud, heavy yet familiar.

"Good morning, sweetie," my mom said cheerfully, her smile attempting to dispel the atmosphere. "How did you sleep?"

"Okay, I guess," I replied, forcing a smile as I poured myself a bowl of cereal. "I was chatting with someone I've been seeing."

"Oh? A friend?" My father asked, looking up from the paper.

"Yeah, sort of," I mumbled, my cheeks warming.

After breakfast, we piled into the car. The engine roared to life, and my father took the familiar route through the neighbourhood. Trees danced in the wind, casting shadows on my thoughts. I stared out the window, letting the sights blur as I strategized for the session ahead. What would I say? Would I unravel like a ball of yarn?

"Are you feeling nervous?" my dad asked, breaking the silence.

"A little," I admitted. It was true, my heart raced at the thought of diving into my struggles, the feelings I often buried so deep no one could find them.

"You know, it's okay to let it out," he said gently. "That's what they're there for."

I nodded but didn't respond. The car ride seemed eternal, punctuated by the sound of the tyres crunching on gravel.

When we finally arrived, I stepped out into the brisk spring air, the familiar building looming before me. I could already sense the weight of the conversation that awaited inside.

As I walked through the doors, I was greeted by the comforting hush of the therapy room. The walls were adorned with calming art, and a cosy chair awaited me, ready for the unburdening. I took a deep breath, each inhale a reminder of the hope I clung to.

"Welcome back," Dr Brittan said with a warm smile as I settled into the chair. "How have you been since our last session?"

I hesitated, how could I convey the complexity of my emotions? The allure of Flo's presence, the heaviness of my mind. I jumbled together in a chaotic symphony. So, I started with the easiest piece: "I've been talking to someone."

"Oh? Tell me about her," the therapist prompted gently.

I found myself animatedly recounting the late-night conversations, the way Flo listened without judgment, the way she sent me memes that always made me laugh, and how she just seemed to get it. As I spoke, I saw a flicker of something in my therapist's eyes perhaps it was recognition, the glimmer of understanding the light that Flo had sparked within me.

As we delved into deeper waters, I revealed layers of vulnerability that often felt too raw to share. The struggle with loneliness, the cycles of self-doubt, how it felt like I was navigating a storm while others seemed to glide by unaffected. But there, in that small room, I also felt the warmth of connection of being heard.7

We spoke for what felt like hours, and by the end of the session, there was a lightness in my chest that hadn't been there before. I realized that, while my mental health journey was tumultuous, little moments like conversations with Flo provided beacons of hope.

As I left the office, the world felt a bit brighter. I reunited with my father in the waiting area, and the car ride home was filled with a silence more comforting than before. I had let go a little and summoned courage I didn't know I possessed.

The sun was beginning to set as we pulled into our driveway, painting the sky in hues of orange and purple. I thought of Flo again, and the anticipation of talking to her later filled me with warmth.

Maybe, just maybe, I wasn't as alone as I had once believed. I had allies in my battle, and I was learning to reach for them.

Later on, that evening after dinner with my parents, I retreated to my room to call Flo. The gentle glow of my desk lamp provided a comforting backdrop as we connected over the phone. We began by discussing my day, particularly my time with Dr Brittan at the therapy clinic. It had been a reflective experience, filled with difficult conversations but also moments of clarity. I shared my thoughts about my progress and the challenges that still lingered, feeling grateful for her attentive ear and the reassurance that comes with having someone who understands.

As we transitioned into lighter topics, the excitement of our upcoming third date at the cinema added a spark to our conversation. We revelled in the anticipation of the film we had chosen, playfully guessing the plot twists and what snacks we might indulge in. Despite the struggles, there was a sense of hope and joy in envisioning our time together.

"It's really late, so see you tomorrow. Good night Felix Jones." She texted.

"Good night Flo" I responded.

Good night Diary!

Day 12

Dear diary the morning of my third date with Florence. I really liked felt both exciting and nerve-wracking. I woke up with a flutter of butterflies in my stomach, eager to spend more time getting to know her. We had planned to go to the cinema around one o'clock, and the anticipation of sharing popcorn and laughter filled the air with a sense of possibility. Before diving into the day's events, I made my way to the kitchen to tell my mum about my plans. She always seemed to sense when I needed a little boost of confidence, and today's breakfast was no exception. As she flipped pancakes and asked about my date, her warm smile helped ease some of my anxiety.

Despite the cheerful atmosphere, it was hard to ignore the shadows that often clouded my mind. I have my own battles with mental health, which can sometimes feel overwhelming, particularly on days when I want everything to go perfectly. As I sat at the table, I tried to push those worries aside and focus on the moment. I reminded myself to take things one step at a time. After all, today was about connection and enjoyment, not perfection. With my mum's encouragement ringing in my ears, I felt a spark of determination.

After breakfast, I made my way upstairs, my mind swirling with anticipation for my date with Florence. The morning sun spilled through the window, illuminating the room as I scoured my closet for the perfect outfit. Each piece of clothing I considered brought a mix of excitement and anxiety; I wanted to make a good impression while simultaneously grappling with my own mental health struggles. The music I played in the background acted as both a distraction and a comfort, wrapping me in familiar melodies that helped drown out my racing thoughts.

As I prepared, I felt the weight of my worries pressing down on me, an unwelcome companion during what should have been a joyous occasion. Despite my inner turmoil, the thought of spending time with Florence filled me with a flicker of hope. I imagined her smile, the way her laughter lit up the room, and how easy it was to talk with her. With each song that played, I clung to that hope, using it as a lifeline to anchor myself amidst the waves of uncertainty. As I finally chose an outfit and nervously walked out the front door, I reminded myself to embrace the moment because I had a date with a stunning girl and she likes me back.

At around one o'clock, the cool evening air wrapping around me like a comforting blanket. The bus stop was just a few streets away, and my heart raced with anticipation. Tonight, was the night I was going to the cinema with florence, the girl who made my stomach do flips every time I thought about her. We had been flirting for a while now, as I waited for the bus, I couldn't shake the feeling that this could be the start of something special.

But beneath the excitement, there was a heaviness that tugged at my mind. My struggles with mental health often felt like a shadow lurking at the edges of my happiness, threatening to cast a pall over moments that should be joyful. What if I said something awkward? What if my anxiety got the better of me, and I spiralled into my own thoughts instead of enjoying her company? I took a deep breath and tried to ground myself, reminding myself that Flo was kind and understanding. She had shared a few of her own struggles with me, and I found solace in the fact that we were both navigating the complexities of our emotions.

As the bus approached, my thoughts raced. What movie did we decide we were going to see? Should I hold her hand or just keep it casual? The possibilities danced in my head, and I willed myself to stay present. This was a chance to connect with someone who seemed to see the real me beneath the surface. Climbing aboard the bus, I felt a mix of nerves and excitement.

The bus rolled to a gentle stop outside the local cinema, its bright marquee lighting up the dusk with promises of adventure and laughter. My heart raced in anticipation as I stepped onto the pavement, the cool evening air brushing against my skin. This was it: the moment I had been waiting for, another date with Florence, someone who had sparked a light in me that I had been missing for so long. The thrill of being with someone I fancied was often overshadowed by the shadows of my mental health struggles. I worried about how I would come across, whether my anxiety would creep in and overshadow the night.

As I made my way toward the entrance, I could see Flo in the distance, her smile brightening the dimming light. She looked radiant, her laughter ringing out as she waited patiently on her phone. Yet, even at that moment, my mind was racing would I be able to engage with her like I have in the past? Would I say something foolish or stumble over my words? I often grappled with this inner dialogue, a persistent echo reminding me of my battles, but I wasn't going to let that stop me from enjoying this night. Holding onto the hope that maybe, just maybe, with Flo beside me, the shadows might fade into the background, if only for a little while.

As I approached her, I took a deep breath and gave her kiss on the cheek, I said "Hi how are you today, I have missed your smile."

"I am having a much better day now I am with you." She said in an excited tone, while her cheeks blushed and turned red.

As we leaned against the cool, brick wall of the cinema, we discussed our favourite films and shared silly anecdotes about movie moments that left us in stitches, I felt a fleeting sense of relief. Flo's ability to listen and engage made it easier to push aside the nagging thoughts that usually cloud my mind. Maybe. That night outside the cinema, under the starry sky and surrounded by the hum of laughter and chatter, I found a glimmer of hope. The sweet scent of popcorn wafted through the air, mingling with the crispness of a late autumn evening. Even though the vibrant ambience surrounded us,

Flo walked beside me, her chestnut brown hair reflecting shades of gold in the lights, her laughter ringing like a melody. She had this way of making the world seem lighter, even when my thoughts felt heavy. We'd chosen a romantic comedy together, a genre that usually elicited smiles and laughter, the kind of movie that would distract me from my worries for a while.

"Do you think they'll serve popcorn with extra butter?" she asked, her eyes sparkling.

"Only if we're lucky," I replied, trying to ignore the uneasy flutter in my stomach. The truth was, while I wanted nothing more than to enjoy the evening, the shadows of my mind often clouded my joy.

We entered the lobby, filled with the sounds of laughter and chatter, the chatter of excited patrons discussing their movie choices. As we stepped into the line at the kiosk stand, I felt a pang of anxiety wash over me. It was a discomfort I had become familiar with: the guilt of feeling out of place, the fear of letting Flo see the darkness that sometimes settled over me.

"Do you want to share a large popcorn?" Flo suggested, breaking my train of thought.

I nodded, grateful for her casual ease. "Sure. That sounds great."

As we took our seats inside the screen room, the lights dimmed, and anticipation filled the air. I felt a flutter of excitement mixed with trepidation. The movie began, but I had trouble focusing. The characters' antics played out before me, but my thoughts drifted to worries the weight of expectations and the fear of disappointment. Would Florence get tired of me? Would I drag her down with my struggles?

Florence, however, was captivated by the screen. I snuck glances at her, watching the way she smiled at the jokes and whispered witty comments under her breath. She didn't seem to mind the occasional moments of silence that fell between us. Yet, even in that dimly lit room, the internal battle raged on within me.

I took a deep breath and tried to push my thoughts aside, letting myself get lost in the story. The characters on screen faced challenges, but they also found light, laughter, and love amid the chaos. It reminded me of Flo, and how she managed to bring warmth into my life even while I was grappling with my shadows.

Toward the end of the film, when the characters shared a heartfelt moment, I felt a glimmer of hope. For a brief moment, all my anxieties faded, and I was simply there with Flo, sharing a laugh over a silly punchline. I softly grabbed her hand and pulled her in for a kiss. She leaned more in and we spontaneously made out in the cinema, which is a first for both of us.

As the credits rolled and the lights slowly brightened, I felt a nudge on my arm. "Hey," Flo said, her eyes searching mine. "What did you think?"

"It was good. Funny," I replied, feeling a rush of gratitude for her presence.

"You know," she began cautiously, "if you ever want to talk about anything like, you know, how you're feeling I'm all ears."

"I am doing much better when I am with you, well, did that take your mind off your cat," I responded "yes definitely, whenever I'm with you, nothing else matters, I feel safe, I feel I am home," Flo said cute and almost fragile way.

I looked at her, my eyes like a lighthouse at night.

"I appreciate that," I said finally, my voice steadying. "It means a lot to me and I have never felt like this, well not in the past few years. I mean you make me the happiest person alive."

As we walked out into the night, the cool breeze brushing against our skin, I felt a sense of lightness beginning to outweigh the heaviness inside me. I didn't have to face them alone. We stepped outside into the colourful blur of Village life, and for the first time that evening, I felt different well, a genuine smile broke through my fears. Maybe it was the magic of the movies, or maybe it was something much deeper, but as we walked together under the glowing streetlamps, I knew that this day was the best day of my life ever, well, yes, it was the best day to date.

After I got home, as I sat in my bedroom, the glow of the streetlights filtered through my curtains, casting gentle shadows on the walls. My heart flutters with excitement as I reflect on my date with Flo at the cinema, which has turned out to be the best day of my life. The film we watched was merely the backdrop to our connection, where every shared laugh and whispered comment felt electric. Holding hands during the suspenseful moments felt like a sweet secret, an unspoken bond that drew us closer. And that kiss light and hesitant at first was a culmination of a beautiful evening that I'll never forget.

Yet, as night blankets my room, the thrill of the day mingles with the familiar weight of my mental health struggles. Moments of joy can feel fleeting, and as I unwind, I grapple with the shadows of my thoughts. The contrast is stark; the happiness I felt with Flo now seems distant, almost surreal. I remind myself that it's okay to experience these highs and lows and that love and connection can coexist with the more challenging parts of my mind. I allow myself a smile, knowing that today brought a flicker of hope into my life, a reminder that there are bright days ahead, even if they are paired with darker nights.

Good night diary!

Day 13

Dear diary the sun peeked through the curtains, casting warm rays across my bedroom as I sat up in bed, the remnants of last night's laughter with Flo still echoing in my mind. Thoughts of her bright smile and the sweet kisses we shared lit up my heart, yet as I swung my legs to the floor, a heaviness settled over me.

I had been looking forward to this morning, to soaking in the warmth of our budding connection, but an impending sense of dread began to envelop me. I tried to brush it off, convincing myself that it was just laziness or the aftermath of a late night. But as I stood up and looked in the mirror, the flicker of anxiety ignited.

My mind spiralled, a cacophony of worries and fears that I had struggled with for years. What if I mess this up? What if I'm not good enough for Flo? The thoughts flooded in like a raging river, pushing me toward a familiar place of panic. I felt my heart race, my palms grow clammy, and before I knew it, I was pacing around my room, a prisoner of my own thoughts.

With each step, the walls felt as though they were closing in on me, my breaths growing shallow and rapid. I could almost hear the ticking clock reminding me that I needed to pull myself together but I didn't know how. My eyes darted around the room, searching for something to anchor me, but all I saw were the remnants of joy from the previous night.

Suddenly, my phone buzzed on the bedside table. I hesitated, almost afraid to look. What if it was Flo? What if I pushed her away with my chaos? The walls feel like they're closing in around me, and I can barely catch my breath. My heart is racing, the pounding in my chest reminding me of the chaos swirling in my mind. The panic attack has taken over, a wave of anxiety that leaves me feeling lost and overwhelmed. I know Flo is messaging me, her concerned texts lighting up my phone, but I can't bring myself to reply. Every time I think about reaching out, the fear tightens its grip on me. I feel like I'm in a dark tunnel with no way out, frantically searching for a breath of calm in the storm.

The pressure of the silence weighs heavily on me, each moment stretching into eternity. I know Flo only wants to help, to pull me back from the brink, but all I can manage is to sit in this turmoil, fighting against the shadows that cloud my thoughts. I should tell her I'm okay, and that I appreciate her concern, but words escape me like whispers in a crowded room. Instead, I wrestle with the spiralling thoughts and the tightening chest, hoping that somehow, this will pass.

Sitting on the floor of my room, I felt the world closing in around me, each second amplifying the chaotic storm brewing within. My chest tightened, and my breaths came in shallow gasps, as though I were drowning in an ocean of anxiety. The walls felt like they were inching closer, and every sound became a cacophony that pierced through the haze of my panic. Just then, the door swung open, and my mother rushed in, her eyes filled with concern and determination to help me find solace. I could see the love in her gaze, but at that moment, I was overwhelmed by the intensity of my emotions.

Despite her calming words and gentle touch, my panic attack had taken the reins, driving me to lash out in frustration. It felt as though I was trapped in a whirlwind, spiralling out of control.

"Leave me alone" I shouted at her, the words pouring out like venom, fuelled by an energy

I couldn't comprehend. In my distorted reality, she was the embodiment of everything overwhelming, and I found myself hurling objects around the room, seeking release from the internal chaos. Each thud of a book hitting the floor seemed to echo my cry for help, but I couldn't see beyond the tempest within me to realize that she was only trying to pull me back from the edge. It felt like the voice inside was more of the protagonist in the situation and I wanted to go away.

As my energy waned, a mix of guilt and regret began to settle in the aftermath of my outburst. I could see the hurt in my mother's eyes, and in that vulnerable moment, I longed for connection, even as my mind battled against it. The storm within me started to ebb, but the damage had already been done. I was left sitting amid the wreckage of my emotions, realizing just how painful it can be to feel trapped in a cycle of fear and rage, and how important it was to find healthier ways to navigate through those turbulent waters.

My room lay in chaotic disarray, a physical manifestation of the turmoil that had engulfed my mind just moments before. Clothes were strewn across the floor, books lay open and forgotten, and the remnants of my emotional upheaval clung to the air like a heavy fog. My mother stood quietly in the doorway, her expression a mix of concern and tenderness as she processed the scene before her. Having just witnessed the raw eruption of my panic, she moved cautiously, offering her comfort in soft words and gentle gestures. But as much as I appreciated her presence, the weight of my emotions felt too dense to share; all I longed for was solitude, a sanctuary where I could retreat and calm the storm that raged within.

With each deep breath I took, I felt the tension in my body begin to loosen an ache that still clung to me like the mess around me. My mother's voice, soothing and melodic, reached me from across the room, urging me to talk, to express what I felt. But I couldn't find the words; I didn't want to dig deeper into the chaos when all I needed was a moment to breathe and let the world fade away. I wanted to cocoon myself in the familiar confines of my own thoughts, to take refuge from the noise outside and allow my mind to settle. The remnants of my panicked rage echoed in my ears, and the thought of sharing it felt overwhelming. All I craved was some quiet, an interlude of peace to reset my cluttered psyche and find my centre again.

After the chaos of the morning's panic attack, I stayed in my room, seeking solace in the soothing embrace of music and the written word. The familiar melodies enveloped me, creating a cocoon that shielded me from the world outside. Each song became a thread, knitting together the frayed edges of my mind, while the pages of my book transported me to different realms, allowing me to escape for just a little while. My mum, always intuitive to my struggles, would pop in every so often, her gentle presence a reminder that I wasn't alone. She'd check on me with a soft knock and a warm smile, her reassurance grounding me in moments of discomfort. I could hear my phone buzzing occasionally, but I chose to ignore it; Flo's messages, although filled with concern and care, felt too overwhelming to confront while grappling with my own turmoil.

At that moment, the outside world faded away as I cantered myself in this fragile peace I was trying to rebuild.

After the chaos of the morning's panic attack, I stayed in my room, seeking solace in the soothing embrace of music and the written word. The familiar melodies enveloped me, creating a cocoon that shielded me from the world outside. Each song became a thread, knitting together the frayed edges of my mind, while the pages of my book transported me to different realms, allowing me to escape for just a little while. My mum, always intuitive to my struggles, would pop in every so often, her gentle presence a reminder that I wasn't alone. She'd check on me with a soft knock and a warm smile, her reassurance grounding me in moments of discomfort. Also, she told me to remember what the therapist and use those techniques to control myself.

I could hear my phone buzzing occasionally, but I chose to ignore it; Flo's messages, although filled with concern and care, felt too overwhelming to confront while grappling with my own turmoil. In that moment, the outside world faded away as I centred myself in this fragile peace I was trying to rebuild.

Good night diary.

Day 14

Dear diary the sun spilled softly into my room, illuminating the remnants of yesterday's chaos. It felt strange to stand amidst the mess I had made clothes strewn across the floor, unwashed dishes cluttering the desk, remnants of my thoughts captured in every corner of my mind. The panic attacks had hit me like a tidal wave, leaving me gasping for air and struggling to keep afloat in a sea of anxiety and despair. But today was different; today I felt a sense of purpose as I began to tidy up, trying to reclaim my space.

As I picked up discarded clothes, I glanced at my phone resting on the bed. A text notification blinked urgently. It was from Flo, and the warmth of her message wrapped around me like a familiar hug. She had asked how I was doing, and in that moment, I knew I needed to reach out, to open up about my struggles more. My fingers hesitated above the screen vulnerability was hard but I took a deep breath and began to type.

"Hey, Florence. I just wanted to let you know I had a panic attack yesterday. It was really overwhelming. I'm okay now, just trying to clean up my space a bit. Thanks for checking in on me."

I hit send, and an unexpected wave of relief washed over me. It felt good to share, to let someone in.

Once I'd cleared most of the clutter, the sunlight flooding into the room felt like a warm embrace. I plopped onto my bed, exhausted but strangely invigorated. Just as I settled in, a knock echoed through the door.

"Hey! It's me!" A cheerful voice floated through the wood. I recognized it instantly: Tommy, my best friend. We hadn't seen each other in weeks. My anxiety had kept me holed up in my room, but the sound of his voice stirred something in me a longing for connection that I hadn't realized I missed so desperately.

"Come in!" I called, almost shyly.

The door swung open, and there he was his infectious smile brighter than I remembered, eyes sparkling with mischief. He stepped into the room, taking in the remnants of my recent battles with mental health and the evident mess of my life.

"Wow, it looks like a tornado hit," Tommy remarked with a grin. "But I'm so glad to see you! How are you holding up?"

"Better," I admitted, my voice slightly shaky. "Just trying to tidy up. I had a panic attack yesterday and it's kind of threw me for a loop."

Without missing a beat, Tommy stepped closer, his expression shifting from playful to sincere. "I'm really sorry to hear that. I've missed you, you know? I've been worried and besides I am board of beating my parents at poker."

"It's been hard," I confessed, vulnerability spilling out like the laundry on my floor. "But I'm working on it. Today feels a bit brighter."

The strange weight of the room lightened as we fell into an easy rhythm of conversation. Tommy had this way of making me feel like I was the most important person in the world. We talked about everything that we had missed in each other's lives, the last movie we watched, the goofy things that had happened in our friend group while I was away. Laughter filled the air, cutting through the heaviness that had enveloped me for so long.

"Wanna help me finish cleaning?" I asked playfully, holding up a pile of clothes as if it were a trophy.

"Only if you promise to play me in at cards after we're done," he shot back, feigning seriousness. "No one cleans faster than me, you know."

We began picking things up together, and as we laughed and joked, I felt the tension in my chest begin to ease. Tommy's presence was like a plane, grounding me in the moment and reminding me I wasn't alone in this fight. My heart swelled with gratitude for his friendship.

"Thanks for coming over, Tommy," I said earnestly as we wrapped up the cleaning, tossing the last of the clutter into the laundry basket. "I really needed this."

"Anytime, bestie. Just remember, you don't have to do this alone," he said, a serious glint in his eyes that made my heart flutter. "Let me be there for you, okay?"

I nodded, feeling the bonds of our friendship strengthen right then and there. Anxiety was an invisible storm, but Tommy reminded me that I had others in my corner, people who would weather it with me.

"Okay tell me now how many girlfriends have you had since we last met Tommy? Also, I hope you're ready to lose at cards," I teased, a smile breaking out across my face, steering the conversation back to lighter grounds.

As we settled down for our gaming battle, I felt a flicker of hope. It was just a day after chaos, after panic, and yet, here I was surrounded by laughter, untangling the knots in my mind with each passing moment. That night after Tommy went home, it reminded me that there was light at the end of the tunnel, especially when you had good friends by your side. Buzz Buzz!! My phone was lit up, so I checked, and Flo replied.

"Hey, how about we meet by the pond tomorrow and just chat? Just remember everyone has good and bad days, but it's how we bounce back from them that counts" she texted.

"Thank you, I really appreciate that" I replied promptly.

Good night diary

Day 15

Dear diary the sun filtered through the curtains, casting warm patterns across my bedroom floor. It was a crisp morning, and despite the lingering echoes of the panic attack that had gripped me two days ago, today felt different. Yesterday, after a long heart-to-heart with Tommy, we had put our past behind us and rekindled our friendship. It was a relief to have that weight lifted off my shoulders.

Flo's text had come through while I was still trying to recover from the chaos in my mind. "Hey! Just checking in. How are you?" It felt like a lifeline, her simple words wrapping around me like a hug. I replied quickly, my fingers dancing over the screen. "I'm okay! Meeting you later at the pond?" She responded with a smiley face, and suddenly the day felt filled with promise.

With determination, I pushed myself out of bed, shedding the remnants of yesterday's anxiety. I stepped into the shower, letting the warm water wash over me, the steam enveloping my thoughts like a cloud. I lingered for a moment, breathing deeply until I felt ready to face the world again.

Afterward, I stood in front of my closet, staring at my collection of clothes a rainbow of choices but none seemed right at first. I wanted something that not only felt comfortable but also ignited a spark of confidence. I finally settled on a soft, oversized sweater vest and my favourite pair of jeans. The outfit felt like a gentle armor, a way to shield my vulnerability while still being myself.

Downstairs, the smell of porridge filled the air, and I was greeted by the sight of my parents sitting at the kitchen table, chatting amicably. "Good morning!" my mom called, a smile illuminating her face. The sound of their laughter grounded me, reminding me that even during stormy times, life continued, anchored by small moments of joy.

I joined them, pouring syrup in my porridge, savouring each bite. They inquired about my plan for the day, and I shared my excitement about meeting Florence. They exchanged knowing looks, happy to see me stepping out and engaging with friends again.

After finishing breakfast, I slipped on my worn sneakers, the soles carrying the weight of many such mornings. The cool air brushed against my skin as I stepped outside, a refreshing balm that seemed to awaken all my senses. I walked briskly down the path towards the park, each step lightening my heart a little more with every breath.

As I reached the park, I spotted Flo sitting on a bench, her hair dancing in the gentle breeze. She looked up and waved, her face lighting up with a smile that mirrored my own excitement. I hurried over, and before sitting down, I threw my arms around her in a long and meaningful hug.

"Long time no see!" she joked, releasing me and folding her hands in her lap. "How are you doing, really?"

I took a moment, consciously allowing myself to acknowledge the fatigue I felt from my recent struggles. "I had a rough patch, but I'm better today. I feel like I'm finally moving forward slowly."

Flo nodded, her understanding gaze reassuring. "I'm really glad to hear that. I'm here for you, you know, anytime."

We started to walk along the pond's edge, the water glimmering under the sun, and my heart felt light as we talked about everything and nothing.

We shared stories, caught up on the latest school gossip, and laughed until our sides hurt. Also, I told how I rekindled my friendship with Tommy. The worries that had once loomed above my head began to dissolve in the warmth of our connection. I couldn't help but think how incredible it was to be surrounded by genuine love, and how much they anchored us in turbulent waters.

As we strolled around the pond, I realized how significant these moments were. With each step, I felt a little more whole. The small uncertainties faded away with the haunting whispers of the panic attack. I was allowed to experience joy again, to laugh, and to deeply connect with those I cared about.

After sharing the tumultuous experience of my mental health panic attack with Flo, I felt an unexpected wave of relief wash over me. She listened intently, her eyes filled with understanding and empathy, and I could see the weight of my words resonating with her.

In that moment, surrounded by the serene beauty of the pond, something shifted between us. Without a word, she leaned in closer, her soft lips brushing against mine in a gentle yet electrifying kiss. The world around us faded away, and all that remained was the warmth of our connection.

We kissed for what felt like an eternity, the sound of water lapping gently against the shore creating a soothing soundtrack to our intimate moment. Flo's touch was tender as if she were trying to convey all the unspoken support and love I desperately needed. I could sense her commitment to be there for me, to help me navigate through the storms of my mental health struggles. Each lingering contact of our lips felt like a promise, an unbreakable bond forming in the heart of the sunset's golden glow. In that enchanting moment, I realized that amidst chaos, beauty could emerge, and love could flourish in the most unexpected places.

As the sun dipped below the horizon, casting a warm golden glow over the local pond, I felt an overwhelming rush of emotion after our kiss. It was as if time had momentarily halted, allowing me to savour the sweet, electric connection we shared. With a heart full of hope and vulnerability, I turned to Flo, my voice barely above a whisper as I asked her to be my girlfriend.

"You make me the happiest person alive," I confessed, feeling the weight of my struggles with mental health lift ever so slightly in her presence. I said "Every day I'm with you is another reason for me to live, I can't imagine my life without you in it. Do... you... want to be my... boyfriend?"

"I love... you more than anything, we both have struggles and we can get through this together. By the way... yes to being your... girlfriend." She replied excitedly.

Those words were more than just a declaration; they encapsulated the tumult tossed within my mind. For so long, I battled my inner demons, navigating through shadows that threatened to engulf me. But in the warmth of our shared laughter and the comfort of her smile, I found moments of clarity that reminded me of the beauty life could hold. Flo was my beacon, illuminating even the darkest corners of my psyche. I hoped she could see how profoundly she impacted my life, how her companionship turned the mundane into magic, and how her love was a gentle reminder that I wasn't fighting these battles alone. Together, we could explore the depths of joy, wrestle with pain, and emerge stronger, cherishing the small, precious moments that life offered us by the pond and beyond.

A rush of emotions enveloped us as we learned in for a long, lingering kiss by the serene pond. The soft sound of water lapping against the banks mirrored the heartbeat of our newfound connection, each moment feeling both exhilarating and comforting.

As we broke apart, the world around us faded into the background, and all that existed was the warmth of her hand in mine. Together, we began our walk home, fingers intertwined, sharing sweet whispers and laughter that echoed through the cool evening air. It felt like we were in our little bubble, a sanctuary where love blossomed amidst the chaos outside.

Despite the joy of being together, there was an underlying struggle within me. The weight of mental health challenges loomed like a shadow, threatening to dampen the brightness of that beautiful moment. I found peace in her presence, but there were times when my thoughts would spiral, overshadowing our happiness. I wanted to be the boyfriend she deserved, yet I grappled with moments of sadness and anxiety. Holding her hand felt like grounding myself, a reminder that I wasn't alone in my battle. As we shared our hopes and fears during that walk, it became clear that love isn't always about perfection; sometimes, it's about supporting each other through the storms and striving for brighter days together.

After a leisurely stroll back to Flo's home, where the gentle whispers of the breeze danced with the rustling leaves, I walked my new girlfriend to her doorstep, my heart racing just a little faster with each step. The golden rays of the setting sun bathed the scene in a warm glow, creating a moment that felt almost magical. When we finally arrived at her house, the world around us faded away, leaving just the two of us in that ephemeral bubble of excitement and tenderness. I leaned in, feeling a rush of emotions swell within me, and pressed my lips softly against hers. The kiss was sweet, filled with promise and vulnerability, and as we pulled away, I could hardly contain the words that had been dancing on my tongue.

"I... love you," I whispered, the sincerity of the moment grounding me in a way I'd never experienced before.

With a sparkle in her eyes and a smile that lit up her face, she responded in kind, "I love you too." Her words held a depth that resonated with my very core, evoking a warmth that wrapped around me like a cosy blanket.

As she stepped back into her house, I lingered in the moment, my heart swelling with joy and anticipation for what the future could hold. The evening air was cool, and the world felt alive with possibility, but all I could think about was that sweet exchange, a simple yet profound affirmation that made everything feel right. Saying goodnight felt bittersweet, but as I turned to leave, I couldn't shake the feeling that something beautiful had just begun, plus I have a girlfriend and she is beautiful.

I couldn't contain the excitement bubbling within me. The evening air was crisp, and our laughter echoed in the streets, leaving me with a warm glow that lingered even after we said our goodbyes. As I hurried back to my room, I felt an overwhelming urge to share this moment with someone who understood me Tommy. I flopped onto my bed and dialled his number, my heart racing with anticipation. I could already picture his enthusiastic reaction as I recounted the little details: her smile, the way her eyes lit up when we talked, and the dreams we shared about the future.

But as much as I wanted to drown in the happiness of new love, there was a shadow looming over my heart. Mental health struggles had been a constant battle for me, often making it difficult to fully embrace moments of joy. I reminded myself that while I revelled in the happiness of my new relationship, I also needed to acknowledge the fears and anxieties that still whispered in my ear. When Tommy picked up the phone and asked how I was doing, I hesitated for a moment, torn between the elation of my new girlfriend and the gripping reality of my mental health. I knew I had to share everything the good, the bad, and the complicated and hoped that my friend could help me navigate this whirlwind of emotions.

"Tommy... Tommy... guess what? I texted.

He replied, "are you ok, ... You had a bad day again."

"Well no! remember Florence "I texted

"yes, the girl from the waiting room" he texted back.

"She is my girlfriend and I have never felt more happier in my whole life," I replied.

"Go on, you get her, I have never been a prouder friend" he texted.

After our conversation, I knew it was time to tell my parents.

As I made my way downstairs, the living room was cosy, the faint glow of the TV washing over the space like a comforting blanket. My parents were curled up together on the sofa, laughing at some sitcom that usually felt mundane, but today, it seemed brighter.

I cleared my throat, the words heavy on my tongue. "Uh, Mom, Dad?" I suddenly felt like a kid again, apprehensive about sharing my report card. "I have something to tell you."

Before I could spill the news, they turned their gazes toward me, their smiles widening. The anticipation in their eyes instantly reminded me of the past, when I would unveil the truth about my struggles. Then it happened they jumped up, grabbing each other's hands and doing an impromptu dance, twirling and stomping in high spirits. My face lit up but quickly turned crimson with embarrassment.

"Oh, come on!" I groaned, burying my head in my hands. "Stop!" I almost cried-laughed, unable to contain the warmth in my heart despite my flooded cheeks.

My parents, oblivious to my amusement-turned-embarrassment, delighted in this spontaneous celebration of my new romance.

"Did you say you're dating Florence?" my mom half-screamed, still dancing while my dad gave a twirling flourish that almost knocked over the coffee table.

"Yes! Yes!" I shouted over their shenanigans, desperately wishing for the floor to swallow me whole. "But do we have to do this now?"

They paused mid-twirl, suddenly serious. My dad stepped forward and clasped my shoulders. "Buddy, this is huge! We're just so happy for you! Florence seems like a wonderful girl!" His sincerity radiated from him, infusing the room with a joyful warmth.

"I know," I finally admitted, that warmth battling my inner turmoil. "I just… I don't know how to handle all of this sometimes."

The laughter faded, and my parents exchanged a knowing look. My mom walked over and pulled me into a gentle hug. "It's okay to feel overwhelmed, honey. We're proud of you, and remember, we're here for you. Good days and bad, we'll always support you."

Their kind words sank in deeper than I expected. Though I often felt the weight of my mental health struggles, moments like this filled with genuine love and encouragement reminded me of the light that could still break through the clouds.

"I love you guys," I murmured into the folds of my mom's sweatshirt. It was a simple moment, but it seeped into my heart, filling the cracks that sometimes felt too vast to repair.

After bidding them goodnight, I retreated upstairs, still grinning. As I crawled into bed, I thought of Flo, her laugh, and the way she effortlessly brought light into my world. I held onto that feeling, allowing it to wrap around me like a comforting blanket as I drifted off to sleep, knowing that each day, despite its challenges, could bring brightness into my life.

Good night diary!

Day 16

Dear diary the sunlight poured through my window, illuminating the scattered remnants of yesterday's emotions and excitement. The nerves coursing through me the night before, fading like a dream upon waking. I lay in bed for a moment, silencing the whirlpool of thoughts that threatened to drown me. The flutter of hope and fear mingled in my stomach.

With a deep breath, I finally swung my legs over the side of the bed, feeling the coolness of the wooden floor beneath my feet. I needed to start the day, to see if this lightness in my chest could remain as real as the rising sun outside.

I trudged downstairs to the kitchen, where the smell of breakfast wafted toward me. My parents were already seated at the breakfast table, chatting amicably over mugs of steaming coffee. My mum looked up and smiled when she saw me, a glimmer of pride in her eyes that made me feel warm despite my ongoing struggles with mental health.

"Good morning, sleepyhead," she said, placing my breakfast in front of me. "I've got a plan for us today."

"Hey," I replied, joining them at the table still trying to wrap my head around the fact that Flo was actually my girlfriend now.

"I think you need a new wardrobe for school. The last time we went shopping, you mentioned you needed some new shirts," she continued, her enthusiasm lightening the atmosphere. I couldn't help but grin at the thought of spending time with her.

"Alright, sounds good," I said, digging into my breakfast, and savouring the golden sweetness. My father chimed in, early morning, eyes sparkling. "Speaking of new uniforms, did you hear that Tommy's been training every day for the championship? He's going to lead them to victory!"

"Yeah, he's been telling me about the strategies he has in mind," I said, trying to keep the conversation flowing, to push away the niggling thoughts that always lurked at the edges of my mind. I knew I had to distract myself, at least for a little while longer.

As we chatted, I found it easier to keep my mind on the present, discussing rugby and school uniforms instead of the shadows that danced in the corners of my subconscious. My dad's gentle encouragement cheered me on. "You should come to a game soon; watching Tommy in action could give you some inspiration for your own studies," he laughed.

"Maybe," I replied, the word escaping my lips before I could remind myself how hard it was to be around people sometimes let alone in a crowd, where all my anxieties seemed to amplify.

After breakfast, I headed back upstairs, my mind slowly shifting gears as I prepared for the day. Making my bed was a small act that helped ground me and provided a sense of order. I took a deep breath, looked in the mirror, and reminded myself of the positives of yesterday Flo's smile, our laughter, and the warmth of connection.

As I rummaged through my wardrobe, I realized that I didn't just need new shirts for school; I needed to find something that represented who I was now, something that felt brave as I began this journey with Flo. I pulled out a few old sweater vests that I felt connected to and a couple of pieces that my parents had brought me that still carried that fresh, store-worn scent, undoubting new beginnings.

Once I was ready, I dashed downstairs to find my mum waiting, her eyes softening as they met mine. "You look great!" she exclaimed, and I felt a flicker of pride. I was still unsure about a lot of things, but I was learning, I was trying.

The car ride to the shops was filled with chatter about everything from fashion to friendship, and for the first time in a long time, I felt connected and somewhat whole again. Despite all the struggles that came with my mental health, little moments like these the excitement of a new relationship, the joy of family, and the sense of purpose were beginning to stitch themselves together into a larger tapestry of hope.

As we pulled into the parking lot, I glanced at my mom, her smile bright and inviting. "Can't wait to help you pick out some shirts," she said, her enthusiasm infectious. As I stepped out of the car, I felt the weight of yesterday's anxieties lift, if only for a moment. With Flo by my side and my supportive family supporting me, I was ready to face whatever the day had in store.

I arrived at the big clothes shop. The sun was shining, casting a warm glow on everything around me, but inside, I felt a twinge of nervousness. School was creeping back into view, and I was in dire need of new shirts. We walked side by side, chatting about the upcoming term, the excitement of new teachers, and the friends I'd see again. It was comforting, but in the back of my mind, I couldn't escape my worries about the classes, the tests, and mostly how I sometimes felt like I didn't quite belong.

As we pushed through the automatic doors, the familiar smell of fresh fabric wafted over us. I picked up a navy-blue shirt and held it against myself, imagining the crisp feel of cotton against my skin.

"That looks nice," my mum said, smiling at me.

I nodded, but underneath my calm exterior, a storm was brewing. School had always been a mixed bag for me. Some days were clouded by my struggles with mental health, where everything felt too heavy and too bright all at once.

We wandered through the aisles, flipping through the racks of shirts as I tried to focus on the task at hand.

"How many do you think you need?" my mum asked, peering closely at the fabric of a long-sleeve option.

"Maybe five?" I suggested, trying to gauge how many days I could stretch that out. J

Just then, out of the corner of my eye, I spotted someone familiar Tommy!

"Hey!" I called out, breaking into a smile as he turned around, his hair a tousled mess as always. "What are you doing here?"

"Getting supplies, just like you," he replied, his voice cheerful. "You ready for the new term?"

I shrugged, trying to mask my unease with humour. "As ready as I'll ever be."

Tommy came over, and we started chatting, moving through the aisles together. It felt easier to breathe with him beside me. He joked about the new subjects we might have, and I laughed along, but deep down, I still felt that knot in my chest.

"Want to help me pick some shirts?" I asked, grateful for the distraction. "I'm hopeless at this."

"Sure!" he said, excitement shining in his eyes. Together, we rifled through the shirts, holding them up to each other like runway models, and it made the shopping experience less nerve-wracking.

Tommy was always good at lifting my spirits. We laughed about how ridiculous some of the patterns were.

"I can't believe people wear this stuff," I exclaimed, holding up a shirt with cartoon dinosaurs all over it. "I'd never hear the end of it at school if I wore this."

After a while, as I settled on a few shirts some plain, some a little more colourful I felt that knot begin to loosen. Tommy's laughter felt like a lifeline, pulling me away from the anxious thoughts that often chased after me.

"You know," he said while we walked toward the checkout, "if you ever feel overwhelmed at school, just remember I'm there too. We can navigate it together."

I smiled at that. It felt reassuring. The confidence I sometimes lacked felt a little stronger with him by my side. "Thanks, Tommy. That really helps," I admitted. It was true. Just knowing that someone understood even without needing to say much, made it easier to deal with the circling fears in my head.

Once we finished shopping and walked back to the car, my mum smiled, holding the plastic bag filled with my new shirts. "Did you have fun?" she asked, looking between me and Tommy.

"Yeah, it was great!" I replied, already feeling the weight of the day lessened.

I felt a strange mix of excitement and anxiousness about the upcoming school year. Tommy stood beside me, grinning from ear to ear as we exchanged thoughts on the gaudy designs of our new backpacks.

"I can't believe we're finally year 11!" he exclaimed, spinning around in a circle, his laughter light and carefree. "This year is going to be epic."

"Yeah, for sure!" I replied, trying to match his enthusiasm. But while I smiled on the outside, my mind felt heavy. I was grateful for the new clothes, but the thought of returning to school loomed over me like a dark cloud. I had been struggling with my mental health for a while now, and while I was trying to stay positive, deep down, I was apprehensive about what the year might bring.

Tommy's mom was already waiting for him at the local coffee shop, a beacon of warmth amidst the flurry of back-to-school shoppers. I waved goodbye to him, feeling a twinge of envy at his carefree disposition. As I walked to my mom's car, I felt a sting of loneliness mingle with the excitement of the day.

The car ride home felt unusually long, bogged down by traffic that seemed to crawl at a snail's pace. The usual banter between my mom and me fell silent as we navigated through the maze of honking horns and impatient drivers. Instead, I leaned forward, my phone in hand, eager to reach out to Flo, my new girlfriend.

I tapped out a quick message: "Hey! Just finished school shopping. Got a groovy new shirt! How's your day going? Any big plans for school?"

Flo replied almost instantly, her enthusiasm jumping off the screen. "Sounds cool! I just got some killer shoes and a couple of cute outfits! I'm really excited but also kind of nervous about the first day. How are you feeling?"

I hesitated, my fingers hovering over the keyboard. I'd been wanting to confide in her about my struggles, but the thought of burdening her with my worries made my heart race. Instead, I wrote, "I'm excited, but you know, it's a lot to think about. You know how school can be sometimes."

Just like that, she sent me a flurry of responses filled with encouragement. "I get it. Just remember, you're not alone in this! And if you ever need to talk, I'm here for you."

A warmth flooded through me, mixing with my anxiety. I managed a faint smile, the connectivity comforting against the growing chaos in my mind. It was nice to know that someone cared.

"Flo is really sweet," I thought to myself, glancing at my mom, who was lightly tapping her fingers against the steering wheel, lost in her own thoughts. Just then, a new wave of traffic clogged the road ahead of us, forcing the car to a complete stop.

"Traffic today is unreal," my mom said, breaking the silence. "How is Tommy?"

"Pretty good," I replied, deciding to keep the tone light. "I got a new backpack and some stuff for school. Tommy is really excited about this year."

"Good! I'm glad you're getting excited too," she said, glancing at me in the rear-view mirror. I could sense she wanted to ask more but chose to let it rest. I appreciated her respect for my space, and that she wasn't pushing me to spill my heart just yet.

As we sat there in the stillness of the car, I took a breath and reflected. At that moment, surrounded by the car's familiar scent and the soft sounds of muffled traffic, I felt a flicker of hope. Maybe this year wouldn't be so daunting after all.

The asphalt stretched ahead of us like the new school year vast and uncertain but with endless possibilities. I glanced down at my phone, the screen vibrating with another message from Flo: "And remember, we can do this together. Let's meet up later today for a walk around the pond?"

That settled it. There were good things on the horizon. I responded with an enthusiastic "Yes! Can't wait!" and smiled as the car finally began to move again. Whatever challenges lay ahead, I knew I wouldn't have to face them alone.

As the car rolled to a stop in our driveway, I could still hear the faint buzz of excitement from the shopping trip. But as soon as I handed her the bags, my thoughts raced ahead like a wild stream   I was about to see Flo, my new girlfriend.

"Thanks for the help, Mom!" I called over my shoulder, already sprinting down the sidewalk towards the local pond. The sun hung low in the sky, casting warm, golden rays that danced on the surface of the water. It wasn't just the beauty of the pond that drew me; it was Flo, sitting there, waiting for me.

When I spotted her, my heart skipped a beat! She was perched on a wooden bench beneath the old oak tree, her wavy hair catching the sunlight, creating playful shadows on her face. I rushed over and enveloped her in a big hug, feeling the warmth and comfort that came from being with her.

"Hey, how are you?" I asked, pulling back to look into her dark, expressive eyes.

"Better now," she replied, a smile breaking through her earlier pensive expression. There was a moment of silence as we both took a seat on the bench, the gentle lapping of the water providing a soothing backdrop to our conversation.

As we settled in, I felt the weight of the past week lift off my shoulders. School was just around the corner, and with it came a storm of anxiety and anticipation. I glanced at Flo, and I could see she felt it too. "So," I started, "what are you most excited about this new year?"

She thought for a moment, her gaze drifting over the rippling water. "Honestly? I'm scared. A new school year feels like a fresh start, but what if I can't handle it? There's always so much pressure to keep up." I could hear the tremor in her voice, and I understood. I felt the same way the weight of expectations pressing down like a heavy blanket.

"I get it," I said softly, feeling a connection form in our shared vulnerability. "Sometimes, it's hard to just keep going, you know? With everything we've got on our plates... Sometimes I just feel like I'm drowning."

"That's how I feel too." Her voice was barely above a whisper, but there was a strength in her honesty. "It's hard to talk about it, but It just feels like I'm in a fog. I really don't want school to add to that."

I reached for her hand, intertwining my fingers with hers, grounding myself in that small, reassuring gesture. "You're not alone," I said firmly. "I want you to know that it's okay to feel how you're feeling. We can tackle it together if you want. I'm here for you."

She looked up at me, her eyes glistening with unshed tears, but there was also a flicker of hope. "Really? That would mean a lot. I'm just worried I'll push everyone away when things get too hard."

"That won't happen. I promise." I squeezed her hand reassuringly. "We can support each other. Let's start a new tradition whenever things get tough, we meet here. Just us, the pond, and a conversation. No judgment, just listening."

Flo smiled, and it felt like the clouds that had been clouding our heads began to part. "I'd like that," she admitted. "Sometimes just talking about it can make it feel a little more manageable."

As we sat there, sharing stories, worries, and laughter, I realized that our love had the potential to grow into something much deeper. We weren't just sharing the weight of our worries; we were building a safe haven for each other amidst the chaos of life and school.

That evening, as the sun dipped below the horizon, painting the sky in hues of orange and purple, I felt a wave of relief wash over me. Together, we might not solve everything, but being there for each other was a good place to start. And under that vast sky, with the pond reflecting the last light of day, we found solace in knowing we would navigate the challenges ahead together.

Flo was standing on the edge, her feet dangling just above the surface of the water, the golden light illuminating her hair. We fell into conversation, laughing about everything and nothing, sharing our dreams and fears about the impending school year. Just as a dragonfly flitted by, I leaned in, and we shared a small kiss. It felt like time paused for a moment, capturing the sweetness of youth and innocence in just a heartbeat.

After the kiss, we walked hand in hand. The familiar trail to her home felt different; everything seemed brighter, more alive.

When we reached her door, I could feel the weight of the evening's conversations lingering in the air. I glanced into her eyes, searching for reassurance and finding it there. I leaned in and planted a kiss on her cheek, a gentle promise that we'd support each other through whatever the year would throw at us.

"Good night, Flo," I murmured, my heart a mix of contentment and the bittersweet wrappings of a day well spent.

"Good night Felix Jones," she replied, her smile glowing in contrast to the dim porch light.

I watched her enter the house, savouring the moment before finally turning for home.

As I walked back, the coolness of evening settled around me, bringing a sense of calm. The familiar path and gentle breeze helped clears my mind. When I stepped through my front door, the enticing smell of dinner wafted through the air. My mom had prepared spaghetti a dish I always looked forward to.

"Hey there! How was the pond?" she asked as I took a seat at the table. My dad was already settled in, a newspaper partially folded to reveal a sports page.

"It was great!" I shared details of our day, the laughter, and the kiss, as my parents exchanged knowing glances. They smiled, their encouragement shining through.

Dinner was filled with stories, the three of us animatedly chatting about my new girlfriend, my mom reminiscing about her own first crushes and my dad chiming in with gentle teasing. I felt grateful for the warmth of home a place where I could always be myself.

Once dinner was over, I helped my parents clean up. The rhythmic clatter of dishes being placed in the sink was comforting. After the last plate was rinsed and dried, I bid them goodnight and made my way to my room.

The dim light of my lamp cast a cosy glow as I settled onto my bed. I grabbed one of the books I had originally intended to read for school, but tonight, it became my escape. As I flipped through the pages, I found my mind drifting back to Flo the way her laughter sounded, the warmth of her hand in mine, and that brief moment by the pond.

Somewhere in those pages, I drifted off to sleep, wrapped in dreams of school, new beginnings, and the quiet promise of more moments like the one by the pond. It was a simple day just shopping and a kiss but somehow, it marked the start of something new, something exciting.

Good night diary!

Day 17

Dear diary the sun peeked through the curtains of my room, casting gentle rays across the messy assortment of clothes and books that lined the floor. Today felt different, brimming with a quiet optimism that I had decided to embrace. Sure, the struggles with my mental health still loomed in the background like a heavy fog, but I held on tightly to the support of Florence and Tommy. They were my anchors in this sometimes-turbulent sea.

After a few moments of deliberation, I settled on a comfortable sweater vest and jeans. It was the scruffy combination that made me feel like myself, a perfect blend of relaxed and ready for the day. I smiled at my reflection, encouraging my mind to quiet the self-doubt that often crept in during moments like this.

Downstairs, the familiar aroma of toast wafted through the air, mingling with the unmistakable crunch of cereal. My parents sat at the kitchen table, sharing stories and laughter that I found comforting. I joined them, pouring myself a generous bowl of my favourite cereal honey nut oats while tuning into their light-hearted banter.

As we chatted, I took a moment to appreciate the simplicity of the moment. My parents were my support system, both genuinely caring about my well-being and a solid reminder that I wasn't alone. With each bite of cereal, I felt a little more grounded, preparing me for the day ahead.

"Excited for book club later?" my dad asked, looking up at me with inquisitive eyes.

I grinned. "Yeah, it's gonna be great this time. Flo will be there."

His eyebrows raised in surprise. "Is this her first time?"

"No! She loves it. We're discussing that new mystery novel," I said, my thoughts drifting momentarily to the way Flo's eyes sparkled when she spoke about stories, her passion for books awakening a similar excitement in me.

After breakfast, I gathered up my things, the energy buzzing within me like electricity, and practically bounded to the front door. Flo was waiting for me outside, leaning against her bike, a wide grin spreading across his face as she saw me approach.

"Ready for a thrilling session of literary debate?" she teased, pushing off from his bike to walk beside me.

"Absolutely," I replied, feeling lighter with every step we took toward the community center where our book club met. Having Flo there always lifted my spirits, her nature and unwavering love reminding me to enjoy the little things in life.

As we arrived, a wave of familiarity washed over me. The cosy room smelled of old books and coffee, a comfortable haven for those who shared our love of stories. The other members were already settling in, scattered around the large wooden table, their discussions igniting a buzz of anticipation in the air.

She looked to me, her eyes lighting up, and I felt my heart match the rhythm of her joy. The day faded from my mind as we all delved into the book, our thoughts weaving together like the pages we had read.

As the session progressed, it became clear that Flo was more than just a pretty face in the room. She articulated her thoughts with an insight that not only impressed me but sparked lively debate among our group. I watched her intently, filled with pride, knowing that she shared a piece of herself in every word.

After the meeting, as we lingered to chat with the others, I found a moment away from the crowd with Flo. "I'm so glad you came tonight," I said, genuinely grateful for her presence.

"Me too," she replied, her voice soft, eyes meeting mine with an understanding that transcended words. "I always have a lot of fun."

Kyle another member of the club, caught a glimpse of us and called out, "Hey, lovebirds! Let's hear your hot takes on the plot twist!" We laughed, the light heartedness wrapping around us like a warm blanket. We were buzzing with excitement, our minds still swirling in the realm of fictional adventures and heated debates about the characters' motivations.

"We should totally ride home together," Flo suggested, her sparkling eyes lighting up at the idea. Her bike, a vintage blue cruiser with a bright red basket, leaned casually against the brick wall. It looked inviting, and as we both hopped on, I couldn't help but feel a mix of thrill and trepidation.

We climbed onto the bike, Mia in front and me wedged behind her. At first, it was a clumsy endeavour, our legs awkwardly entangled as we tried to find a rhythm. Pedalling together was like attempting a dance where the steps were constantly out of sync. We laughed at our struggle, the sound mingling with the rustling leaves around us.

"Okay, on three! One… two… three!" I called out, and we attempted to steer in sync. It was hilariously chaotic; each wobble and swerve sent us into fits of giggles. The world around us blurred into a soft watercolour, imported with the laughter that spilt between us as we pedalled along the sun-drenched path.

But just as we started to gain a little bit of confidence, everything unravelled. Without warning, the bike veered too far to the left, and I instinctively shifted my weight. Time slowed as we sensed the impending fall, both of us clinging to each other and shouting in delight and disbelief. Then thud!

We tumbled to the ground in a heap of arms and legs, the bike collapsing beside us. For a moment, there was silence, but that silence was quickly broken by peals of laughter echoing through the tree-lined path. Flo's laughter was infectious, and soon I was giggling uncontrollably.

"Are you okay?" I managed to ask, still gasping for air between chuckles.

"More than okay! That was amazing!" she exclaimed, between fits of laughter as she swatted at a leaf stuck in her hair. Once the laughter began to die down, I turned to face her. At that moment, our eyes met, and in a burst of sweetness, laughter melted away into a soft gaze. Without really thinking, I closed the gap between us, leaning in to press my lips softly against hers. It was tender, and somehow, everything else, the fall, the bike, and our struggles faded into the background.

When we finally pulled apart, we were both still grinning like goofballs, but the world felt a bit different. Just a little lighter. We embraced, the warmth of the moment wrapping around us, cutting through the heaviness that often lurked in the shadows of our minds.

"Okay, let's walk the bike back. I think we both could use a little more stability tonight," Flo said, still half-smiling, and I couldn't agree more.

We took turns holding the handlebars, each step filled with light-hearted banter as we made our way down the path. With the bike on one side and each other on the other, we strolled together, sharing our thoughts about the book, our hopes, and even our struggles.

Flo had always been open about her mental health journey, sharing stories of the challenges she faced. I had my share as well, but during moments like these the laughter, the kisses, the trust exchanged with every step-in sync, I found solace and an unspoken promise of support in our togetherness.

As twilight began to settle, the stars peeked through the veil of dusk, each one a reminder of the light we could find even amid the chaos. We arrived at her house, breathless from laughter, slightly bruised, but alive with joy.

"Same time next week?" she asked playfully as we leaned the bike against the porch.

"Definitely, However, let's walk next time" I replied, knowing that whatever obstacles came our way, we could ride through them together.

The warm glow of the streetlights flickered through the branches of the trees as I walked Flo home. The evening air was crisp, but the delightful buzz from discussing our latest read kept us warm inside. We laughed about the characters and debated their decisions, the conversation flowing easily like a favourite song.

When we reached her house, Flo expertly manoeuvred her bike into the shed next to her house. The soft click of the shed door echoed in the darkness, and I could see the faint outline of her smile as she turned back to me. The world around us faded for a moment, and it felt like time had paused, just for us.

"Can you believe how predictable that ending was?" Flo remarked, her eyes shining with enthusiasm.

I chuckled, leaning against the fence. "I know! I was hoping for a twist, but I guess some authors stick to formulas."

We continued to chat for a few minutes, the excitement of reading and sharing our thoughts creating a bubble of joy around us. Just then, her mother called from inside, her voice breaking our reverie.

"Florence, sweetie! Time to come in!"

Flo sighed and shot me a playful look. "Duty calls." She stepped closer, and our lips met again for a brief, soft kiss. It was sweet, lingering, filled with a promise that this would not be the last we'd see of each other tonight.

"Good night," I whispered, my heart fluttering as I watched her retreat toward the door, where her mother waited with an expectant smile.

The walk back to my house felt a little longer than usual. The falling leaves crunched under my feet, and the night air, cool and crisp, was interspersed with the scent of wood smoke from nearby chimneys. I thought about Flo, the way she laughed, how her eyes sparkled when she talked about the characters in our book, and how every moment with her felt like an adventure.

Once I reached home, I slipped off my shoes and padded into the living room, the comforting sight of my parents relaxing on the couch greeted me. They looked up, curious and expectant.

"Hey, how was it with Flo at book club?" my dad asked, his eyes bright with interest. My mom offered a warm smile, eager to hear the details.

"It was great," I replied, settling into the armchair across from them. "We had a really good discussion made me think about the book in a whole new way."

"Did you two get a chance to talk afterwards?" my mom asked, her tone teasing.

"Yeah, I walked her home," I added with a grin, feeling a rush of warmth in my cheeks.

My mom clapped her hands together, clearly delighted. "Young love! It's so sweet. Alright, let's order pizza tonight can't be bothered to cook!" she announced, glancing at my dad who nodded in agreement.

I shared their excitement, though I was also a little hungry. "What do we feel like eating?" I asked, already reaching for my phone.

"Pepperoni for me! And make sure to get extra cheese!" my dad chimed in.

With a few taps on my phone, I placed our usual order: a large pepperoni and extra cheese with a side of garlic knots because why not? As I set the phone down, I felt that familiar warmth again the kind that comes from being with family and the thrill of new love.

The conversation flowed easily, my parents sharing stories from their own dating adventures, and I couldn't help but smile at how life seemed to repeat itself in these little moments.

Soon, the doorbell chimed, and the tantalising smell of pizza wafted into the air as my dad made a beeline for the door. As we gathered around the dining table, I felt grateful for the simple pleasures, the warmth of home, the joy of Flo, and the comfort of good food shared with loved ones.

After the delightful pizza night with my family, the laughter, the crunch of crusts, and the bubbly cheese, I had volunteered to take the empty boxes out to the bin. The cool evening air brushed against my skin as I stepped outside, breaking the warmth of our kitchen. It felt good to contribute, even in the small way of tossing cardboard into the bin, a reminder that little responsibilities could lend a sense of normalcy amidst the chaos of my thoughts.

Once back inside, I hopped into the shower. The warm water washed over me, soothing my shoulders as the steam enveloped the bathroom. I closed my eyes, if only for a moment, trying to forget the heaviness clinging to me the weight that seemed to follow me everywhere. With a deep breath, I turned up the music in the background. A favourite playlist filled the air with melodies, gently pulling me away from the darker corners of my mind.

I danced. Just a little shimmy and sway, but in that moment, I felt a flicker of joy. There was something liberating in the rhythm, the way the music wrapped around me like a soft blanket. It reminded me of better days, of times when I used to dance more before the cloud of uncertainty decided to linger in my thoughts.

After the shower, I dried off and wrapped myself in a clean, comfortable T-shirt. I settled into bed, picking up the book I had been trying to read. It was a good story, one that had captivated my attention moments before my mental health struggles pulled me into a fog. I opened the pages, determined to escape reality for a little while, but the words blurred together, just like the thoughts in my head.

Just as I began to lose hope in my book, my phone buzzed beside me. It startled me out of my reverie. I picked it up, half-expecting a notification that would create a new wave of anxiety, but instead, it was Flo.

"Hey you, what's up?" Her message glowed on the screen, a little beacon of warmth in the dim light of my room.

We chatted about everything and nothing here, little jokes about our favourite show, and random thoughts that popped into our heads. It felt comforting to connect with her, to share laughter over silly memes and puns. For a while, I forgot about the nagging worries that plagued me, drifting along the current of our conversation.

As the night wore on, we shared our struggles to the anxiety and the doubts that crept around the edges of our lives, tightening like a coat too small. She never judged; instead, she understood, and in that understanding, we found solace in each other.

"I'm glad we can talk about this," Flo said, her words flowing through the screen, finding the little crevices where hope needed to be. "You're not alone, remember?"

And for those moments, I believed her. I believed we could share the burdens sometimes if only to lighten my load.

Our chatter slowed as fatigue set in. Yawning, I glanced at the clock and realized how late it had gotten. It was time for bed, both for me and for Flo. We said our goodnights, and as I tucked myself in beneath the covers, I felt a strange mix of emotions. I was grateful for the conversation, and for her unwavering support, yet I still knew that the shadows were there, just waiting in the corners of my mind.

As sleep finally began to drape its heavy curtain over me, I reminded myself that tomorrow is another day. Perhaps one that would shine just a little brighter, guided by the flickers of hope and kindness woven through moments spent with the people I loved.

Good night diary!

Day 18

Dear diary as I sat at the breakfast table, the morning light streamed in through the kitchen window, illuminating the cosy space where my family gathered. The smell of toasted bread and freshly brewed coffee filled the air while I absentmindedly picked at the cereal in my bowl. It was a usual day meant for relaxation if only I could shake off the lingering cloud that hung over me.

"Morning' sweetie," Mom said, setting down her mug as she caught me staring out the window, lost in thought. "You okay?"

"Yeah, just feeling a bit down, I guess." I fiddled with my spoon, tracing circles in the milk. "Flo's at her grandparents' and Tommy's busy with rugby practice. I guess I just feel kind of… alone."

Dad looked up from his paper, concern etched across his face. "It's alright to feel that way. We all have our ups and downs." He reached out across the table to squeeze my hand. "But you're not alone, you know that, right?"

I nodded, appreciating their support but still feeling that emptiness tugging at me. "I know, but sometimes it feels overwhelming. And school is just around the corner. I don't want to think about that yet."

Mom set her hands on the table, leaning in closer. "How about you take today for yourself? No pressure to think about school or anything. Just relax and do what you enjoy."

I let out a small smile; her words wrapped around me like a warm blanket. "Yeah, you're right. I'll just chill in my room today, watch some movies or read."

"Well, that sounds perfect. Just let us know if you need anything," Dad added, his voice steady and soothing.

After breakfast, I retreated to my room, feeling a mix of gratitude and sadness. I didn't want to feel more disconnected, scrolling through social media while everyone else was busy with their own lives.

Instead, I opened my bookshelf, scanning the spines of my favourite novels. I settled on one comforting story I'd read multiple times. As I curled up in the corner of my bed, the words washed over me, transporting me to another world where problems felt distant and easily solvable.

Time slipped away, and soon I heard the faint sound of laughter outside. I peered out the window and saw a group of kids playing soccer in our backyard. Memories flooded back of my own carefree days spent running around, laughing with friends, lost in the moment. A pang of longing hit me again.

The morning light poured through my window, casting a warm glow over my room. I stared aimlessly at the walls, my mind a chaotic swirl of thoughts that seemed to tangle like the cords of my headphones. The familiar heaviness settled in my chest an unwelcome companion that never quite seemed to leave. After battling it for hours, I finally reached for my phone, desperate for a distraction.

Flo's name lit up the screen, a beacon of comfort amidst the fog. I smiled as I read her message: "On my way to my grandparents'! Ready for a long drive. Talk to me?" My heart lifted slightly as my fingers danced across the keyboard, sending a quick reply.

She sounded cheerful, her excitement palpable even through text. I could picture her in the passenger seat, sunlight catching her hair, the breeze of the open window playing with the strands. I didn't tell her about the heaviness I felt; I wanted her to enjoy her journey, unfettered by my clouds.

The conversation flowed effortlessly, and it felt like old times before life settled its burdensome weight on our shoulders. Flo spoke about her grandparents, the stories they told, and how her grandmother's pies were the stuff of legends. Laughter punctuated our texts, a rhythmic beat that made the minutes fly by. With each message, I was pulled further from my thoughts, and the barrier between me and the outside world momentarily dissolved.

Time slipped away, and before I knew it, the screen flashed a message: "Almost there! Love you!" I felt the familiar pang of bittersweet joy. I adored our talks, but I also knew what it meant our moment would soon end.

I responded with a quick "Love you too! Can't wait to hear all about it later!" and settled back into my room, the quiet pressing down once again.

With a sigh, I glanced at the stack of books on my nightstand. They were my escape, the portals to worlds far removed from my own. I picked one up, the cover soft under my fingers, and opened it to a random page. Words leapt off the page, characters springing to life, yet my mind felt glued to my worries. I read the same line over and over, but the narrative slipped through my fingers. The weight of the world was too much some days, and today felt particularly heavy.

As if sensing my struggle, I propped the book against my knees and reached for my phone again. I scrolled through our past conversations, the snapshots of our lives intertwined in texts. I found comfort in the flurry of selfies, the plans nestled within emoji-filled messages. Her laughter seemed to echo behind each screen, a reminder that hope could exist even amid darkness.

I set the phone down, closed my eyes, and took a deep breath, conjuring Flo's voice in my mind. I thought of how she always found the silver linings, how she danced between the raindrops of life with grace. "You've got this," she would say, her voice like honey. "It's okay to take a break."

With that thought, I set the book aside and decided it was time to get some fresh air. I pulled myself off the bed, feeling the fabric of my emotions cling, but I pressed forward. I ventured outside, welcomed by the gentle breeze that whispered promises of better days ahead.

The world beyond my room was alive with colours and sounds, the laughter of children playing in the distance and the hum of leaves rustling overhead. I took a moment to breathe, inhaling deeply, letting the fragrance of blooming flowers soothe my senses. The warmth of the sun wrapped around me like a comforting hug, dispelling a bit of the weight that clung to my heart.

I began to walk, my thoughts billeted between the beauty around me and the challenges that lie ahead. I knew the journey with my mental health wasn't linear, but every small step was progress. I reminded myself that it was okay to feel low but also essential to reach for the light, like Flo reaching for the stars in the night sky.

As I made my way down the street, my phone buzzed again another message from Flo. I smiled as I opened it. "Just arrived! Can't wait for Grandma's pie and stories. We'll catch up later?"

I replied quickly, "Enjoy! Can't wait to hear everything."

In that moment, I understood that though the shadows might linger, they wouldn't define me. I had my own light in Flo, and together, we could navigate the ups and downs. The world felt a little brighter with my small steps forward, and deep down, I knew I was worth fighting for, one day at a time.

The soft hum of the evening was a gentle reminder that life continued on just outside the walls of my small, cluttered room. A stack of books lay haphazardly next to my bed, their pages waiting to be turned while sunlight, now fading, streamed through the half-drawn curtains. I wrapped myself in a worn blanket, relishing in its familiarity as the weight of the day pressed down on me.

Just as I settled in, my phone buzzed, breaking the quiet's hold. It was Mia. I picked up with a smile, her voice bright and cheerful, a spark that lit up my dimly lit room.

"Hey! I'm on my way back from Grandma and Grandpa's," she said, her laughter spilling through the receiver. I could almost picture her in the car, sunlight streaming through the windows, her hands casually steering while the other gestured animatedly as she spoke.

"How was it?" I asked, eager to escape the confines of my own mind, if only for a moment.

"Oh, you won't believe the stories they told me! Grandpa was showing me his old war medals. He's got this incredible one from Korea," she continued, her voice brimming with excitement. As she spoke, I could hear the sounds of the road behind her, the gentle whoosh of the tires mingling with her animated retelling of family tales.

Flo told me about the backyard gatherings, the smell of barbecue mingling with laughter, and how her grandmother had pulled her aside to teach her the secret to the perfect chocolate chip cookies. I envisioned the warmth of socks pulled high, the crackle of golden leaves outside as autumn settled in, and the way her eyes sparkled with every exaggerated gesture she made when recalling a funny family mishap.

With each anecdote, my heart felt a little lighter, her joy infecting me even through the phone. But the heaviness in my chest remained, the dark clouds of my mental health gathering, ready to rain down doubt and anxiety. I tried to push the thoughts away, focusing instead on her laughter, but they lingered, shadows clawing at my tranquillity.

After we spoke for nearly an hour, Flo finally said, "I'll be home soon,"

"Yeah, that sounds great." I felt a small flicker of hope as we said our goodbyes, but the moment she hung up, I was enveloped once more by the solitude of my room. I decided to distract myself with a movie something light, something that would hold my mind captive.

The TV flickered to life, casting a warm glow across my room as I browsed through recommendations. I settled on a comedy, something silly and easy to digest. For a while, I got lost in the storyline, laughing at the outrageous antics of the characters on the screen. But soon, as the movie continued, the laughter faded into a gentle buzz, and the vibrant colours slowly began to blur.

I felt my eyelids getting heavier, and before I knew it, I had drifted off to sleep. In dreams, there was no weight on my chest a world where I could escape the suffocating thoughts that often engulfed me. I dreamt of laughter, of familial gatherings that mirrored Flo's stories, bright and filled with love. The sound of her voice wove through my dreams, pulling me like a lighthouse beacon.

Good night diary!

Day 19

Dear diary the sun peeked through the thin curtains, casting diagonal stripes of light across my room, but the glowing rays couldn't penetrate the heaviness in my chest. It was another morning, and I woke up feeling more stressed than the day before. The thought of school starting again loomed over me like a dark cloud, a reminder that routine would soon reassert its dominance.

For weeks, the anticipation of being back in that environment had gnawed at my insides, each tick of the clock pulling me closer to a reality I wasn't ready to face. My mental health had started to deteriorate again, spiralling into a familiar abyss that whispered self-doubt and anxiety. I rolled over, staring at the ceiling, searching for some semblance of peace amid the chaos in my head.

Eventually, I dragged myself out of bed. The familiar rattle of my phone shattered the silence I saw Flo's name light up the screen. With a sigh of relief, I texted her, asking if she wanted to come over today. I wasn't up for the outside world, not when my heart felt so heavy.

"Sure! I'd love to," she replied almost instantly, and I felt a flicker of warmth in my chest. Mia always had a way of chasing the clouds away, even if it was just for a little while.

I quickly got dressed, the mundane routine of pulling on a sweater vest and jeans oddly comforting. As I made my way downstairs, the aroma of coffee greeted me. My parents were already in the kitchen, chatting over breakfast. I could see the steam curling up from the coffee pot, a familiar sight that usually brought comfort. Today, though, it felt like I was about to step onto a stage, my heart racing at the thought of introducing Mia to them.

"Hey, Mom. Dad," I said, plopping down at the kitchen table. They looked up, their smiles warm, but I felt a lump in my throat.

"What's up, honey?" my mom asked, her tone inherently soothing.

"I, um…" I hesitated, fiddling with the edge of the table. "I invited Florence over to hang out today." It wasn't just a casual invitation; it felt monumental, like revealing a piece of myself I had kept hidden.

Both my parents exchanged glances, a hint of curiosity sparking in their eyes. "Your girlfriend?" my dad asked, his voice steady but gentle.

"Yeah, she's great," I rushed to add, hoping to express just how much she meant to me. "I've been feeling pretty stressed lately, and I thought having her here might help." My voice softened at the last part, almost as if saying it out loud made it more real.

"Of course! We'd love to meet her," my mom said, her tone brightening. "Just let us know when she arrives."

As I munched on a piece of toast, a troubling knot still lingered in my stomach. What if they didn't like her? What if their expectations clashed with the reality of who Florence truly was? But even as those thoughts spiralled in my mind, I could also feel a sense of relief knowing I wouldn't have to face the day alone. Mia was my pillar when everything felt rocky, and having her there would make it somehow easier.

I finished my breakfast quickly, my thoughts racing with snippets of our time together, each memory a reminder of the laughter, the comfortable silence, the connection that always made the world feel a little less heavy. Checking the clock, I realized it was almost time for her to arrive.

Just as I placed my plate in the sink, the doorbell rang, and I felt a jolt of excitement mixed with trepidation. My heart hammered in my chest as I walked to the door, and when I opened it, Flo stood there with a bright smile, her hair catching the morning light.

"Hey!" she chirped, her energy radiating warmth.

"Hey," I replied, stepping aside to let her in. "I'm glad you could come."

My parents were right in the living room, and I felt Mia squeeze my hand as we walked in together. "Mom, Dad, this is Florence," I introduced, a slight tremor in my voice still there, but Flo's presence grounded me.

"Nice to meet you," Flo said, her voice steady and confident, even as she stood before my parents.

"The pleasure's all ours," my mom replied, her smile wide and inviting.

As they chatted, I stepped back for a moment, watching them engage over small talk about school and plans. For that brief moment, I felt a wave of gratitude wash over me a feeling that perhaps today wouldn't be as heavy as I had feared.

Flo caught my eye and winked, and I knew in that instant, no matter what the world through our way, we would figure it out together. The sun slipped higher into the sky, and for the first time in what felt like ages.

The sun streamed through the living room windows, casting a warm glow over our small home. My parents had just met Florence, my new girlfriend, and as we exchanged polite smiles and casual small talk, I felt a surge of excitement mixed with anxiety. Flo was everything I had hoped for funny, bright, and surprisingly open about her own struggles.

"Okay, we're going upstairs now!" I announced, trying to muster some confidence as I took Flo's hand.

My mom looked up from the couch, a teasing smile on her face. "Just remember, door always open, please!" she called after us.

I rolled my eyes, but it was a familiar reminder of our family's openness.

Once in my room, I left the door behind us. I could finally breathe without the pressure of my parents' scrutiny. Flo looked around curiously, taking in the scattered books and the messy remnants of my hobbies. I stepped closer, leaning in to share a kiss. It felt electric the kind of moment that ignited something deep inside me, a reassurance that, for now, everything was okay.

After a few moments, we pulled away, both of us smiling shyly. "So, what do you want to do?" I asked, trying to steer away from the weight of my usual thoughts.

"Are you any good at poker?" I asked, my eyes sparkling.

"Not as good as I'd like to be," she admitted with a laugh.

"But I can teach you if you'd like to learn!" I replied

"Okay, I'm in!" she said.

I rummaged through my desk drawer and pulled out a deck of cards, shuffling them absentmindedly as I sat on the edge of my bed. She perched next to me, her demeanour as relaxed and playful as ever. I dealt out the cards and began to explain the rules, trying to mask the heaviness that sometimes clouded my thoughts. Flo listened intently, and I could see her enthusiasm growing as I explained the strategies behind each hand.

"You know," she said, biting her lip as she looked at her cards, "I've never really played card games before. I always thought they seemed so complicated."

"I get that," I replied, "but it can be a lot like life. You have to read the room, know when to hold on and when to let go."

She raised an eyebrow at me. "Is this a metaphor for something? Because I think I get it."

I laughed, feeling the tension in my chest lighten a bit. "Well, yeah. If I'm holding onto bad cards the bad thoughts that try to pull me down I have to learn when to let them go and draw some new ones."

Flo watched me closely, her gaze unwavering. "You're really brave, you know that?"

Her compliment threw me off guard. "Thanks. But it's not always easy. I struggle a lot with my mental health. Some days, I feel like I'm just up against a wall."

"That makes sense," she replied softly. "I do too. Sometimes I feel like I'm stuck in my own head, and I don't know how to get out."

"That's exactly it," I said, encouraged that someone else understood this complexity. "But being here, with you, feels different. Like I'm not alone in this. You give me hope to find my way through it all."

She smiled, her eyes reflecting a sincerity I longed for. "Let's help each other then. Deal?" as she leaned in for another kiss, holding me tight, clinging to me like ivy.

As we resumed our game, Flo's laughter filled my room, intertwining with the cautious optimism growing within me. The poker game felt less like a battleground and more like a safe space, where challenges could be tackled in each round we played and shared.

With each hand dealt, as Flo glanced up at me, I felt myself opening up a little more, loosening the grip I usually had on my worries. Her presence unplanned yet inevitable began to reassure me. We may not have known every strategy in poker or how life really worked, but in that moment, surrounded by the chaos of a card game, we found a little bit of clarity together.

We found solace in each other's company, sharing thoughts mingled with laughter and gentle moments of silence. Outside, the world was tinted in the soft glow of the setting sun, the sky painting hues of orange and purple that seemed to echo the warmth between us.

"It doesn't feel real, does it?" Flo said, looking up at the sky. "Sometimes I think things are too good to be true."

I paused, giving her hand a reassuring squeeze. "It might sound cliché, but I believe we deserve the good things in life, especially after all the tough stuff. You know I'm here for you, right?"

Flo nodded, her eyes reflecting vulnerability mingled with gratitude. "It's just hard sometimes… to separate the good from the bad in my mind. I wear my smiles like shields, but I've been feeling like they don't hold up much anymore."

After spending the rest of the day in my room with my girlfriend Mia, our laughter and playful banter had filled the space with warmth. The poker game had ended, and though I lost more rounds than I won, it hardly mattered. What mattered was the way she smiled, the light in her eyes as she teased me over a poor hand, and the way we sank into a comfortable silence, side by side on the bed, wrapped in each other's embrace.

As evening fell, our conversations drifted from trivial anecdotes to deeper topics. We talked about our hopes, our dreams, and the shadows that often loomed over them our worries about the future, the pressure of school, and the persistent weight of mental health struggles that both of us battled with in our own ways. More than once, I found myself sharing fears I had kept hidden for years, while Mia listened intently, her hand warm and steady in mine.

"There's something about being here with you that makes it a little easier," I admitted, squeezing her fingers gently. "Like I'm not alone in this."

Flo looked at me, her expression softening as she brushed a stray hair behind her ear. "You're not alone, and you never have to be. I promise."

The evening grew late, and soon it was time for Flo to head home. The thought of parting stung more than I expected; it left a hollow ache in my chest. As we stood up from the bed, I insisted on walking her home, despite her protests. "I can manage," she said lightly, but I could sense the weariness beneath her words.

Once we reached the front door, my parents were there to say goodbye. "It was lovely to finally meet you, Florence!" they said with warm smiles.

It felt good to see my parents embrace her with such kindness, to feel that connection merge seamlessly between our families. Flo waved goodbye, her cheeks flushed with a hint of embarrassment, but her eyes sparkled the same spark I adored so deeply.

We laced our fingers together as we stepped outside, my heart racing not just from the cool evening air but from the allure of her presence beside me. Under the canopy of streetlights, we walked slowly, talking about everything and nothing. Our laughter echoed in the stillness of the night, our shoulders brushing, our fingers intertwined.

The conversation took a poignant turn as we approached the last street before her home.

"Sometimes, it feels like I'm stuck in this fog," she admitted softly, her voice almost lost in the whispering breeze. "Like I'm moving, but I can't see where I'm going."

I nodded, letting her words sink in. "I get it. The world can feel so overwhelming, especially when you're fighting these battles on your own."

She looked up at me, her face illuminated by the golden light of a nearby lamp. "But when I'm with you, it's like… it fades a little. You help make it lighter."

The vulnerability in her words made my heart swell and break all at once. I leaned closer, brushing my lips against hers softly. "You're brave, Florence. Even on the days you don't feel it, you're still fighting. And I'll always be here for you, ready to face it all together."

With the distance to her house shrinking, our pace slowed further. We lingered outside her front gate, wrapped in each other's embrace.

"Promise me you'll take care of yourself, even when it feels impossible," I murmured, tucking a loose strand of hair behind her ear.

She smiled, a gentle, hopeful smile that ignited my spirit. "I promise. And I'll remind myself that it's okay to ask for help. Just like you've done."

As I stepped back, ready to say goodbye, I drew her in for one last kiss, one filled with all the unspoken words promises of support, laughter, and love. In that moment, it felt as if the weight of the world had lifted just a little bit.

"Goodnight," I said softly.

"Goodnight Felix Jones," she replied, turning towards her door but then pausing. "And don't forget I'm here for you too. Always."

As she stepped inside, the soft click of the door echoed in my mind, and I walked home alone, yet not lonely. The night sky above was filled with stars, and I felt a flicker of hope ignite within me. Together, we would navigate the fog. Together, we would face whatever came next.

Good night diary!

Day 20

Dear diary the sun streamed through my bedroom window, casting long shadows across the floor as I stood in front of my closet, contemplating my outfit. I had always found comfort in choosing what to wear; it was a small act of control in a world that often felt chaotic. After minutes of deliberation, I settled on a soft, oversized sweater and a pair of well-worn jeans. The sweater enveloped me like a security blanket, its gentle fabric easing some of the tension coiling within me.

Downstairs, the familiar sounds of home greeted me. My dad was in the kitchen, perched on a stool, a lightbulb in one hand and a slight frown etched on his face as he twisted and turned it, trying to get it to fit just right. It was a routine morning, the kind I had grown to appreciate. My mom sat at the breakfast table, her coffee steaming in front of her, flipping through a magazine absentmindedly while her fingers traced the rim of her mug.

"Good morning, sweetheart," she said, looking up and giving me a warm smile.

"Morning!" I replied, my voice slightly muffled by the weight of the day ahead. I wasn't quite ready to confront the emotions swirling inside me.

I poured myself a bowl of cereal, the clattering of the spoon against the bowl breaking the silence. My dad finally secured the lightbulb with a satisfied grunt, brushing his hands together and turning his attention to me. "Almost ready for school?" he asked, hopeful.

I nodded, forcing a smile that didn't quite reach my eyes.

After breakfast, I helped my mom wash the dishes. The warm water felt soothing against my hands, and for a brief moment, I let the rhythm of scrubbing and rinsing distract me. With each plate I cleaned, I felt like I was washing away a bit of my anxiety.

"You know," my mom started, her tone casual but her gaze thoughtful, "if you ever want to talk about anything school, friends, or if you just need a break, we're here for you."

"Thanks, Mom," I said, grateful for her support but feeling the familiar tightness return in my chest. I wanted to talk, but words often felt like stones lodged in my throat, heavy and unyielding.

Once the dishes were put away, I trudged back upstairs to finish getting ready. I could hear my parents' soft chatter drifting up from the kitchen as I closed my bedroom door. Standing in front of the mirror, I scrutinized my reflection. Underneath the sweater, I felt the weight of anxiety pressing down on me a reminder of the struggles that persisted each day.

As I caught sight of the small, framed picture sitting on my bedside table. It was from last summer, during a camping trip with my friends. We were gathered around the fire, laughter lighting up our faces as the flames danced in front of us. That moment felt like a world away now, overshadowed by the thoughts that played on repeat in my mind: What if I didn't belong? What if no one noticed me?

At that moment, I felt a surge of determination. I took a deep breath. This was my final therapy session before the school year started a safe space to share my fears and frustrations. My therapist, Dr. Brittan, somehow always knew how to untangle the mess of thoughts inside my head, and I hoped today would be no different.

Before I left the house, I slipped the photo into my backpack, determined to bring it up during therapy. I needed that reminder, that happiness wasn't just a moment frozen in time; it could be something I reached for again.

The crisp morning air brushed against my cheeks as I walked to the car. The day ahead was filled with uncertainty, but I felt just a bit stronger, a little less weighted down. At that moment, I chose to believe that with each step, I was moving toward understanding myself a little more and, perhaps, learning to honour my struggles as part of my story.

I was ready to face whatever came next. The engine hummed softly under me, the vibrations reverberating through the worn seats of my dad's old car. It was an unremarkable ride just a familiar stretch of asphalt lined with trees, slowly transitioning from green summer leaves to the vibrant flickers of early autumn. I stared out the window, watching the world pass me by, feelings of anticipation and dread swirling in my chest.

"Almost there," Dad said, glancing over at me. Worry lines creased his forehead, and I could tell he wanted to ask how I was feeling, but instead, he focused on the road, the morning sun catching hints of silver in his hair.

I picked up my phone again, fingers hovering over the screen. I opened a message thread with Flo it was easier to express myself through texts. With her, I didn't feel the pressure of eye contact or the fear of seeing pity in someone's eyes.

"Last session before school. I'm trying to feel good about it, but I don't know how I will manage." I texted.

I hit send, biting my lip as I waited for her to respond. The memory of last year flooded back, a heavy weight I thought I'd left behind. The laughter that echoed in the hallways felt more like a sinister chorus than a joyful song. The whispers and snickers, days filled with anxiety, and evenings spent hiding from the world. I was still recovering, still standing on shaky ground.

Flo's reply came swiftly.

"You've made so much progress though! Remember what your therapist said? You are stronger than you think!" she replied

Her words brought a small flutter of hope.

I said, "I guess… but what if it's just as bad as last year? I can't do that again. I just want to fit in, you know? Be normal?"

I could almost imagine her rolling her eyes at my self-doubt.

"Normal is overrated! You're already amazing as you are. Besides, I'll be right there with you!" she texted.

I smiled, grateful for her unwavering support. She was like a lighthouse guiding me out of the stormy sea I often found myself in. With Mia at my side, I felt braver.

"Who are you texting?" Dad asked, trying to keep the conversation light.

"Florence," I replied, keeping my gaze on the passing trees. "Just… talking about therapy."

He nodded slowly, tapping his fingers on the steering wheel. "It's good to share, you know. I'm proud of you for going to therapy. It takes a lot of courage."

"I guess," I mumbled, knowing I was pushing back the weight of my worries, yet it felt good to hear him acknowledge my effort.

Just then, my phone buzzed again.

"Just a reminder You don't have to face school alone! And if things get tough, text me! I'll be there right away. I promise!" she said.

My grip on the phone tightened; she was right. I didn't have to face everything alone, even though sometimes the weight of isolation felt too much to bear.

"Dad?" I asked suddenly, my voice catching in my throat. "What if school is just as bad this year? What if the bullying starts again?"

He cleared his throat, a hint of sadness in his eyes. "I'd like to think it will be different. You've got support this time. And even if things get tough, we'll tackle it together, okay? You're not alone."

I nodded, though uncertainty still curled in my stomach. The brief silence was only broken by the soft music playing on the radio. I glanced out the window, suddenly noticing an elderly couple walking hand in hand, smiling at each other as they strolled down the sidewalk. A small flicker of determination sparked within me. Maybe I could find my own slice of happiness, too maybe I could learn to stand tall.

As we pulled into the therapy centre's parking lot, I took a deep breath, trying to centre myself. Flo's message echoed in my mind, her words reaching me even through the anxiety that always threatened to engulf me.

"Thanks, Flo. That helps. I'll text you after. Love you!" I replied.

I pressed send and felt a tug of warmth in my chest. As Dad parked and turned off the engine, I realised that this was just one session, one chapter in a larger story. I was still writing my narrative—even with sketchy pages and jagged edges, I had to keep turning the leaves and keep moving forward.

"Ready?" Dad asked, and I nodded, taking his hand for a brief moment before stepping out into the uncertain world ahead. The sky overhead was broad and blue—an invitation, an open canvas waiting to be filled with new experiences.

Together, we walked towards the building, with whispers of hope and determination fluttering in my heart as I stepped inside.

I fidgeted with the fraying ends of my sweater vest, my heart thumping in my chest like a drum. Today was my last session before school started, and while I tried to convince myself that I was ready to walk back into those hallways, I felt anything but confident.

My dad sat beside me, leafing through a magazine that was clearly five years too old to hold any real interest. I glanced at him, his gaze focused on the colourful pages, oblivious to the storm brewing in my mind. He was supportive, always there for me, but some part of me wished I could turn to him and say, "I'm scared," without him having to drop the magazine and try to fix everything.

After a few fleeting moments, my name echoed down the hallway a gentle call that shattered the silence and pulled me from my thoughts.

"Here we go," I muttered, more to myself than to my dad. I could feel his encouraging nod as I stood and walked towards the therapist's office, a realm where I would untangle the knots of my mind yet again.

As I settled into the too-familiar chair, I glanced around the room. The walls were painted a calming blue, adorned with abstract art that, once soothing, now felt like little distractions from the whirlpool of anxiety swirling in the pit of my stomach.

"Hey, it's good to see you again," Dr Brittan, said with a warm smile. he always had this way of making me feel like I wasn't fighting my battle alone, even when I sometimes felt like an island in my own thoughts.

"Yeah, you too," I replied, lifting my gaze to match hers.

"So, let's talk about what's been happening in your life," she prompted, settling back in her seat with a notepad poised on her lap.

I launched into a story about my new girlfriend, Florence. The way her laughter filled the air around her felt like a melody, and how nervous I was when I first held her hand. I recounted the sweetness of our shared smiles, the adventures we had, the late-night texts that filled my chest with anticipation. But beneath all that joy lay the fear that hung over me like a dark cloud—how would school affect our time together?

"And Tommy? How's he doing?" he asked, glancing down to jot something in her notes.

"He's doing great," I replied, my heartbeat easing a little. "He's captain of the rugby team this year. He really deserves it. He's been my best friend since forever, and I know he will lead the team to the championship."

I felt a flicker of pride for him, but it was muted by the anxiety creeping back into my chest like a shadow. "But what if the boys at school start bullying me again? What if the spotlight on him only makes me more of a target?"

Dr Brittan nodded, his expression gentle yet firm. "It's natural to feel that way, especially after what you've been through. But remember, you're not the same person you were last year."

I exhaled a shaky breath, allowing her words to wash over me. "I know, but it's hard. What if I can't handle it? What if the bullying starts again? It messed me up last time, Dr Brittan." I clenched my fists, fighting the urge to let my nerves spill over into tears and show him the picture I packed from my table.

"Let's focus on that, then. What helped you rise from that last experience?" he asked, keeping his voice steady.

I thought for a moment. "Talking to you helped. And Flo… she makes me feel safe. When I'm with her, I forget about everything else."

"Exactly. You have supported this time with the people who care about you. I want you to remember those moments of joy you have with Florence and the confidence you have in your friendship with Tommy. Those can be your anchors when things start to feel overwhelming again."

Dr Brittan's words settled in, creating a base of strength beneath my anxiety. As the session progressed, I shared my worries about classes, the looming pressure of exams, and my struggle to balance everything while keeping my mental health intact.

Eventually, I left that room with more than just a clearer mind but also a plan like a shield to protect myself during the coming school year. He had given me tools to manage my anxiety: breathing exercises, grounding techniques, and, most importantly, reminders of gratitude for the things that filled me with joy.

As I walked back to my dad in the waiting room, I felt a strange mix of optimism and apprehension. I had a choice to make. Sure, school might be daunting, but so was the prospect of letting my fears dictate my life again.

"I'm proud of you," my dad said as we walked out together, the sun bathing us in its forgiving light. It was the first real compliment he had given me in a long time, and I felt a flicker of hope kindle within me.

"Thanks, Dad," I said, a small smile creeping onto my face. "I think I'm ready."

And in that moment, with my dad's steady presence beside me, I felt ready to face whatever awaited me in the new school year. It wouldn't be easy, but for the first time in a long while, I believed I had the strength to try.

The car hummed gently as it rolled down the familiar streets, the sun casting long shadows across the pavement. I stared out the window, letting my thoughts drift to the vivid images from my therapy session earlier that day. It hadn't been easy. My therapist had dug deep, peeling back the layers of stress and anxiety that had settled in like a heavy fog. We spoke of life, my struggles and aspirations and the start of a new school year looming just a few weeks away. Mixed in with all that weight, though, was a lighter subject that brought a smile to my face: Flo.

My dad glanced over, concern etched in the lines of his forehead. "You okay back there?" he asked, his voice steady, a mix of love and worry.

"Just thinking about Florence," I replied, a slight smile tugging at my lips. "We're going to the meet again soon. I can't wait."

He nodded, his gaze returning to the road. "That sounds nice. You two should have a great time."

When we finally pulled into the driveway of our modest home, I could see our neighbour, Mr Jackson, out front, his old lawnmower wheezing as he cut his grass, the smell of freshly cut grass filling the air. Dad parked the car and turned to me. "I'll be right back. Just going to chat with Mr. Jackson."

"Okay," I said, already opening the door. I rushed inside, a wave of relief washing over me as I felt the comfort of my own space beckoning.

"Mom!" I called out as I stepped through the doorway, my voice echoing in our cosy living room. I found her in the kitchen, apron on, stirring something that filled the house with an inviting aroma.

"Hey, honey! How was therapy?" she asked, looking up with genuine interest.

"It was hard," I admitted, leaning against the counter, "but good, I think. We talked about a lot of stuff. School's coming up… just a lot is weighing on me."

She nodded, her expression softening. "I'm proud of you for going, even when it's tough. Want to talk about it more over dinner?"

I shook my head, wanting to retreat into my fantasy world where worries faded away. "I think I just want to relax for a bit. I'll talk later."

"Okay, sweetie. Just remember I'm here if you need anything," she called after me as I headed to my room.

Once the door clicked shut behind me, it felt like the world outside faded. I dropped my bag onto the floor and sank into my chair, the familiar crinkle of pages beckoning me. I reached over and grabbed my book, a tattered copy of a fantasy novel that had become my escape route.

As I settled in, I turned on my music, letting the melodic notes wash over me. The singer's voice intertwined with the intricate plot of dragons and distant lands, and my mind began to weave tales of bravery and adventure. I imagined myself as the hero of my own story, facing daunting challenges but ultimately emerging victorious.

Every now and then, thoughts of Flo interrupted my daydreams. I envisioned us wandering the fair together, sharing cotton candy and riding the Ferris wheel, the world spinning around us as we laughed, oblivious to everything but each other.

The sound of laughter pulled me from my reverie; it was Dad outside, still chatting with Mr. Jackson. I could hear them talking about the last family barbecue, the usual neighbourly banter I had grown accustomed to. The warmth in my heart swelled as I smiled, knowing that beyond the walls of my room, life was moving forward.

But here, nestled among my books and music, I had my own universe to explore. Here, I was the architect of my dreams, and though therapy may be hard, I was learning to construct bridges over the chasms of my worries.

As the music faded into the background, I lost myself in the page again, ready to embrace wherever my imagination would take me, even if just for a little while.

However, the light of the setting sun couldn't chase away the heaviness that lingered within me after my therapy session. The air felt thick with the weight of my thoughts as I slumped on the couch, phone in hand, scrolling through an endless feed of worries and anxious musings.

I hesitated before tapping Flo's name. She had become my lifeline, my refuge in times of turmoil. As the call connected, her bright smile illuminated my screen. Even through the pixels, I felt a wave of comfort wash over me.

"Hey, you!" she said, her voice filled with warmth. "How was therapy?"

I sighed, the weight of the day pressing down on my chest. "Tough. We talked about a lot... especially about school starting again. I just—" I paused, gathering my thoughts. "I'm scared. I don't want to go back to that environment. I don't want to be bullied again."

Flo's expression softened, and I could see her brow wrinkle with concern. "I understand. That sounds really hard. But you're strong, and you're not alone. You have me, remember?"

A weak smile tugged at my lips. "Yeah, I do."

We spoke about everything: the future, my fears, her dreams, and the things we wanted to do together. Flo always had a way of weaving words into a tapestry that made the world seem a little less daunting. She shared her own worries, too, creating a soothing balance between us. It felt like we were both holding onto each other's vulnerabilities, creating a safe space free of judgment.

Eventually, I suggested we watch a movie together. "Let's escape for a little while," I proposed, and Flo agreed wholeheartedly. We both settled into our separate rooms, the familiar comfort of shared experiences a balm to my anxious heart.

"On three?" I counted down, and with synchronised clicks, we pressed play.

The film flickered to life, but our focus lingered more on each other than the screen. With every humorous line and dramatic scene, we found moments to laugh and chatter about everything from the characters' ridiculous choices to our favourite snacks.

"Did you see that?" I exclaimed as a character made an outrageous decision, prompting a fit of giggles from Flo. "I would never do that!"

"Oh, come on! You know you'd totally go for it," Flo teased, her eyes sparkling with mischief.

Hours melted away as we talked over the movie, sharing stories, hopes, and sometimes silence that felt comfortable rather than heavy. It was like we were connected by a thread, no matter the distance. Eventually, the clock ticked closer to midnight, and I noticed the fatigue creeping into my bones.

I yawned, stretching my arms overhead. "I guess I should probably go to bed now," I said, my voice laced with both weariness and reluctance to end our evening.

"Yeah, we probably should," Flo replied, but even her voice carried a hint of sadness at the thought of hanging up. "But promise me you'll text me when you wake up, okay?"

"I promise," I assured her, a smile creeping back onto my face. "Goodnight, Flo."

"Goodnight, Felix Jones!" she replied, her voice like a gentle caress.

As I ended the call and turned off the light, a sense of peace enveloped me. The shadows in my room no longer felt as daunting, and though the uncertainty about school lingered at the edges of my mind, I felt strengthened. Tomorrow was a new day, and while I was still scared, I knew I didn't have to face it alone. I closed my eyes, letting the comforting hum of our conversations play in the back of my mind as I drifted into sleep, hopeful for what lay ahead.

Good night diary!

Day 21

Dear diary the morning sun peeked through my window, casting playful shadows across my room. I rubbed my eyes and took a deep breath, the weight of another day pressing down on me. The start of the new school year loomed closer, like an impending storm, causing my anxiety to flare. I reached for my phone, and after a moment's hesitation,

I tapped out a "Good morning" message to Florence. We'd been dating for a while now, and I had promised her I'd text her first thing. It felt good to keep that promise, even on days when everything else seemed so heavy.

Just as I hit send, my phone buzzed again. It was Tommy.

"Hey, can we meet at the pond today? I need to talk." It caught me off guard, didn't he have rugby practice? I glanced at the time. He must've cancelled or decided it could wait.

 I quickly typed back, "Sure, I'm free. What time?"

After we settled on three o'clock, I reluctantly got out of bed and dressed. The sunlight splashed across my room, illuminating the clothes that lay strewn across the floor, remnants of my indecision the night before. I settled on a simple hoodie and jeans, comfort over style - that's how I rolled these days.

Downstairs, breakfast was a familiar scene: the smell of cinnamon from the cereal filled the air, mixed with the faint aroma of the lavender fabric softener my mom loved. She was busy folding laundry while Dad sat nearby, absorbed in his newspaper. I plopped down at the table and poured myself a bowl, the crunch of cereal momentarily distracting me from my swirling thoughts.

My dad glanced up from his reading and asked, "What's new, champ?" His casual tone always eased me, even when I didn't feel like talking.

"I'm meeting Tommy at the pond later," I responded, trying to sound casual. "He wants to talk."

My mom looked up, her brow slightly furrowed. "Is everything okay? Is he alright?"

It struck me how parents often absorbed their children's worries as their own. I nodded, trying to brush her concern aside.

"He's fine, just... stuff." I wasn't sure if I would explain the nuances of mental health struggles to her, not today.

After breakfast, I stared out the kitchen window, lost in thought. The pond where Tommy and I spent countless afternoons was just a few minutes' walk from our houses. As kids, we'd spent hours playing, dreaming up adventures, and letting the water reflect our carefree laughter. But now, it felt different more like a place of weighty conversations rather than light-hearted escapism. The sun streamed through the window, casting warm golden rays across my untidy room.

After breakfast with my parents, the comforting sound of clinking dishes had faded into the background, replaced by the hum of my own thoughts. Each piece of clothing strewn about and every unmade bedspread whispered of a mess I'd let linger too long. But today was different. Today, I wanted to clear more than just the physical space I needed to clear my mind.

I turned on some music as I picked up stray socks and replanted the books that had huddled in a disorganized pile. My mental clutter mirrored my surroundings: a jumbled mess holding shadows of worries and fears that refused to leave me alone. After a while, the room looked presentable, but that didn't seem to lighten the haze that had settled over my thoughts.

Waving off those concerns, I dialled Flo on my phone.

"Hey," I said, my spirits lifting a little just at the sound of her voice. We talked about the usual, the ridiculous school gossip and the way her old cat use to always slept in the sunniest spot of the house. Eventually, I brought up my plans to meet Tommy.

"He says he has something big to tell me," I reported, curiosity tinged with trepidation. "I hope it's nothing serious." I bit my lip, wondering if my anxiety was projecting.

"Whatever it is, you can handle it," Flo encouraged a soft calmness in her tone that settled a bit of the storm inside my head. "Just remember, I'm rooting for you. You're stronger than you think."

We exchanged a few more words, her laughter like a balm on my worries, before saying our goodbyes. After our conversation, I felt a little lighter, as if I had shared the weight of my heart with her.

I slipped on my shoes, the familiar tug of laces grounding me in the moment. "I'm heading out!" I called to my parents as I descended the stairs. They waved back, their smiles warm but their eyes bordering on distracted, possibly lost in a world of their own worries. It was a silent understanding; we carried our burdens in our own ways.

The walk to the pond was one I knew well. Each step felt rhythmic, almost therapeutic, as I passed familiar sights the weathered fence, the old oak tree, and memories of laughter with Tommy that layered like the paint on a long-abandoned barn. The air was crisp, filling my lungs as I shrugged off the fading tendrils of anxiety with each breath.

When I finally reached the pond, I spotted Tommy near the water's edge, his silhouette slightly hunched, his hands tucked deep into his pockets. He looked up just as I approached, his eyes reflective of something deeper than our usual light-hearted banter.

"Hey man," he greeted, though his tone wasn't as cheerful as I expected. "Thanks for coming."

"What's up?" I leaned against a nearby tree. The calm ripples on the pond moved quietly as if they sensed our conversation weighed heavier than the sky above, filled with drifting clouds.

Tommy took a deep breath, his gaze steady on the water. "I've been going through a hard time," he said, the admission weighing heavily between us. "I… I think I'm struggling with some changes. I feel really overwhelmed, and I didn't know how to talk about it."

"Hey, you okay?" I asked, glancing at him. I could tell something was on his mind. Tommy was my best friend, the kind of guy who lit up a room without even trying. His charming smile had drawn the attention of countless girls in our small town, and I was constantly in awe of his effortless ability to connect with people.

"Yeah, I just… there's something I've been wanting to tell you," he said, finally looking up at me with a mixture of trepidation and resolve in his eyes.

I could sense the weight in his voice, and my heart sank a little. Having been wrapped up in my own mental health struggles for months now my anxiety, the dark cloud that sometimes felt like it would consume me, I hadn't been there for him the way I should have. I had lost sight of the vibrant person that was Tommy beneath the cool facade he wore.

"What is it, tell me?" I prompted gently, biting my lip as I tried to keep my tone light.

"It's just… I… I'm gay," he said, his voice almost a whisper. "Like, I like men. More than just friends."

I blinked, surprised. It was as if the world had shifted beneath my feet. The air around us felt electric, and for a brief moment, time seemed to freeze. The Tommy I thought I knew, the charming guy who was always surrounded by girls, suddenly seemed like a stranger. But as I looked at him, really looked, I saw the same familiar sparkle in his eyes, his courage shining through the veneer of uncertainty.

"You're kidding," I said slowly, processing the information. "You… you like men?"

"Yeah," he replied, his voice gaining strength.

"I do. I know this is a lot, especially since I've never said anything before, but it doesn't change who I am. I'm still me, and I really hope it doesn't change our friendship."

A rush of emotions swept over me. I felt a swell of pride for him; he was brave, more than I think I could ever be. Thoughts raced through my mind a whirlwind of confusion, acceptance, and support.

"It doesn't change anything for me, Tommy. You're still my best friend, and I'm proud of you for saying this out loud. Seriously, it takes guts and whatever happens at school or through social media, I am here for you."

His shoulders slumped a bit, and the tension that filled the air slightly lifted. The corners of his mouth turned upward into that familiar smile, the one that said he felt a little lighter.

"Thanks," he said, his tone a mix of relief and joy. "I was worried you'd think it was weird or that I'd be different now."

"Why would I think that?" I responded, puzzled. "You're still you. Besides, I've got my own stuff going on, too."

I paused, aware of the storm brewing inside me. "I mean, I can't always be the friend I want to be lately. My mental health… it's been rough. But I want you to know that I'm here for you, man. Like, no matter what."

"Really?" he asked, his expression softening.

"Of course. Just promise me one thing."

"What's that?"

"Let's not let either of our issues make us distant. I can be a bit of a mess right now, but I want you to feel comfortable with sharing what you're going through, too. We're in this together, right?"

He nodded vigorously, a glimmer of excitement in his eyes. "Absolutely. Together."

We sat there in silence for a moment, our shoulders nudging together as we both gazed at the pond. The water glistened under the changing light, mirroring the transformation in our friendship. I realized that while both of us were navigating tricky waters, this conversation had brought us closer.

"Hey," I said, turning to him with a teasing smile, "now that you've told me your secret, does that mean you'll finally stop letting me win on poker nights because it's boring always winning?"

Tommy burst out laughing, the previous tension dissolving into the evening breeze. "One time! I only let you win one time!"

"Yeah, and I just had good cards!" I replied, mock-seriously.

As we descended into light-hearted banter, I felt a warmth bloom in my chest. We were navigating our own individual battles, yet somehow, we were discovering new depths to our friendship. Tommy's revelation about being gay had sparked something precious, and I knew that whatever came next, we would face it together. The sun was setting, casting a warm golden glow over the trees as I dashed through the local woods, my heart racing with a mix of nostalgia and joy. The familiar scents of oak and damp earth filled the air, and for a moment, it felt like we were kids again, lost in a world of imagination and laughter. But this time, there was a deeper significance to our play.

Tommy had come out to me just a few minutes earlier, his voice trembling but resolute, the words heavy with the weight of years spent grappling with his identity. When he told me he was gay, I felt a swell of pride for him. It wasn't easy for him, and I knew it. It had taken courage to face the world in all its fickleness, to be true to himself, but he did it. Tommy was free.

As we chased each other through the underbrush, I couldn't help but grin. He darted past a cluster of bushes, and I quickly followed, laughter spilling from my lips.

"You can't escape me, Tommy!" I shouted, climbing an old oak tree, my childhood instincts kicking in with each step.

It felt good to be carefree again, if only temporarily. Beneath the vines, he rolled his eyes playfully, his laughter infectious.

"Is that the best you can do?" he called out, a teasing glint in his eyes. That glint reminded me of the kid I had grown up with the one who could find happiness even in the darkest of times and whose laughter could brighten any room.

After a good while of evading each other, we finally collapsed on the soft mossy ground, breathless and happy. Tommy lay back, eyes fixed on the sky, watching the clouds drift lazily as dusk began to weave its shadows.

"Thanks for doing this," he said softly, breaking the comfortable silence. "It felt... normal. I needed that."

I turned my head to look at him. There was something peaceful about his expression like a load had been lifted off his shoulders.

"Of course, man. You deserve to feel like yourself." I was genuinely happy for him, yet, beneath the joy swirled a darker undertow a reminder of my own internal struggles. My mental health hadn't been great lately, and though I hid it behind a smile, I felt like a tidal wave of waves just waiting to crash down.

As the sun began to dip below the horizon, painting the sky with hues of orange and pink, I knew it was time to go home. I stood up, brushing the dirt from my jeans, and reached my hand down to Tommy, helping him to his feet.

"Come on Let's get out of here," I said, my voice thick with emotion.

I wrapped my arms around him in a tight hug, squeezing him as if I could transfer some of my admiration and pride into him.

"I'm so proud of you, Tommy. For being you. For being open."

"And I'm proud of you, too," he replied softly, pulling away and looking me in the eyes. "You always know how to lift me up."

I smiled, but inside, I felt a twinge of guilt. I wanted to tell him more about my struggles, about the battles I fought daily that never seemed to fade, but I didn't want to take the spotlight away from him. Today was about celebrating a victory a victory that he fought for so desperately.

As we walked side by side on the trail back home, the stillness of the woods enveloped us, and I couldn't help but feel a sense of hope brewing in my chest. Tommy's journey gave me strength; if he could stand proudly in the face of adversity, then maybe, just maybe, I could too.

With every footstep, a small part of me started to believe that healing was possible. I had my best friend by my side, and that made all the difference. At that moment, I chose to focus on his brightness while holding tightly to the thought that mine would come, one day at a time. Together, we would find our way through the woods.

I stepped away from Tommy's house, the air filled with the sweet smell of spring blooms. Just moments ago, we had shared an important moment, one that marked the beginning of a new chapter in Tommy's life. As the words left his lips, I could see the tension ease from his shoulders, a sense of freedom washing over him that I knew was profound.

After our heartfelt conversation, filled with laughter and tears, I hugged him tightly, feeling an overwhelming surge of pride. Tommy, my best friend since childhood, had shown incredible courage in being true to himself. It must have been a monumental challenge, one that I could only imagine. And yet, he had done it he took that leap, and I was honoured to have been part of that moment.

With my heart swelling, I raced home, excitement coursing through me like a river.

"Mom! Dad!" I called out as I burst through the front door. My parents were in the kitchen, where the aroma of dinner mingled with the sounds of my little brother playing in the living room. They turned, concern flashing across their faces at my sudden entrance.

"What happened? Is everything okay?" my mom asked, wiping her hands on a dish towel.

"Yes! Everything's amazing!" I exclaimed, taking a breath to calm my racing heart. "Tommy just came out to me as gay!"

There was a moment of stunned silence before a grin spread across my mom's face. Dad chuckled, understanding the weight of what I had just said. They exchanged a knowing glance, and then my mom was sweeping me into her arms.

"That is wonderful!" she exclaimed, her voice bright and warm. "We love Tommy! We always have. Just think of how brave he must feel!"

Dad joined the embrace, lifting me off the ground as he swung me around in a joyous circle. "This is great news! We're really proud of you both Tommy for being himself and you for being such a supportive friend!"

Warmth filled my chest as I hugged them back, feeling a rush of happiness that pushed aside my usual anxieties. In that joyous moment, my own struggles felt distant. I had battled my own mental health issues endless cycles of worry and self-doubt, but now, everything faded into the background as love and acceptance took centre stage.

"I knew it was hard for him," I said, stepping back and looking into my parents' eyes. "But now he can be himself, you know? He's free."

"That's exactly right," Dad replied, his voice steady and reassuring. "And he needs people like you in his corner, always. Just think, this is a turning point for him and for you. It's a celebration of who he is."

We shared stories about Tommy, reminiscing about the silly moments and the challenges he faced. "Tommy's finally being true to himself," I explained, and I felt my heart swell again with pride. "He's gay, and it's amazing!"

My father's face brightened. "This awesome! Does this mean he can come over more?"

I laughed, the sound light and bright, my worries evaporating. "Yes! Of course!"

As we gathered around the dinner table, a feast of love and laughter, I felt the weight lift a little more. Sharing in Tommy's triumph not only fortified our friendship but also reminded me of the incredible power of acceptance and love.

My own mental health struggles could wait, at least for tonight, while I celebrated with my family the beauty of authenticity and courage.

That evening, we talked and laughed late into the night, and I couldn't help but feel the warmth of hope blossoming within me a reminder that, even in the face of our inner battles, there are moments of connection and joy that can light the path forward. And I knew, for both me and Tommy, this was just the beginning.

That evening, as I sat on the edge of my bed, the lingering emotions from my unforgettable day wrapped around me like a warm blanket. Tommy, my best friend since childhood, had confided in me, revealing a part of himself that had remained hidden for years. His courage was inspiring, and I felt an overwhelming sense of pride. The rugby captain, the jokester, and the guy who always seemed effortlessly confident had trusted me with his truth, and I vowed to support him in any way I could.

With my heart still racing from the conversation, I pulled out my phone and texted Flo. She had been my rock through my own battles with mental health, always encouraging me to express my feelings and supporting me this past year when so much had felt heavy. Within seconds, my phone chimed with her reply.

"OMG! That's amazing! Tell me everything!"

I smiled, my heart lifting a little as I thought about how my news would thrill her. We had shared so many moments, and Mia had always encouraged me to be open-minded. The idea of Tommy coming out was something she would take to heart.

After a few minutes of texting back and forth, I decided it was time to call her. Flo picked up on the first ring, her voice bright and full of energy.

"Hey! Can you believe it?! Tommy is gay!" I exclaimed, trying to mask how stunned I still was by the revelation.

"I mean, I kind of had no clue, but wow! He came out to you? How does he feel?" she asked, her tone enthusiastic yet poignant.

"He's relieved, I think. It's like taking a huge weight off his shoulders. I'm just so proud of him for being true to himself. I can't believe he trusted me with that."

"That's so special. You should be proud of him, and of yourself! You're such a good friend," she replied, and I could hear the warmth in her voice. "We need to do something to celebrate this something fun!"

"What do you have in mind?" I asked, my intrigue piquing.

"What if we all head to the arcade? You, me, Tommy, and Evie! We can make a day of it! I know how much both of you love playing those racing games and air hockey!"

Evie was Flo's best friend. The idea resonated within me, casting aside my earlier worries.

"That sounds perfect! Tommy and I would love that. I'll ask him if he's up for it."

"Definitely!" Flo said. "And I can already picture the fun we'll have. Just imagine the four of us laughing and competing!"

We chatted excitedly about our plans, and I could feel the efficiency of my mental health lifting bit by bit. Flo's encouragement and enthusiasm reminded me that moments like these are what life is about supporting friends, enjoying experiences, and creating memories.

Once our call ended, I dialled Tommy's number. It rang twice before he picked up, his voice a little hesitant but genuine. "Hey, man."

"Tommy! Guess what? Florence and I are planning a day out to the arcade, and we want you to come along. Evie, Florence's friend will be joining too," I said, sensing a surge of excitement creeping into my voice.

"That sounds incredible! I could definitely use some fun. I'm in!" he replied with an energy that contrasted sharply with his earlier vulnerability.

As I hung up the phone, I felt a rush of joy bloom in my chest. Plans were in motion, and my world felt a little brighter. The thought of standing beside Tommy someone who had weathered every storm with me made me realize how lucky I was. My worries didn't vanish entirely, but they dimmed against the prospect of laughter and camaraderie.

Good night diary!

Day 22

The morning light poured into my room, casting soft shadows on the walls. As I lay there, memories of last night swirled in my mind. Tommy, my best friend, had come out to me as gay. I felt a rush of warmth for him; he had taken a leap of faith, a huge step to share such an intimate part of himself with me. I was grateful that he felt he could trust me. It was both a relief and a responsibility, one that I took seriously.

I reached for my phone and quickly texted Flo. "Good morning! Hope you have a great day!"

I hit send, a smile creeping across my face as I imagined her response. It was nice to have her by my side; she always knew how to lift my spirits.

After scrolling through my social media feed for a bit, I reluctantly swung my legs over the side of the bed and stood up, stretching my arms overhead. Today, I wanted to look good. I rummaged through my closet, finally settling on a soft blue sweater vest and my favourite pair of jeans. As I dressed, I couldn't help but wonder how Tommy was feeling this morning. I hoped he was doing okay; I knew it could be daunting to come out, especially when navigating high school politics.

As I made my way downstairs, the comforting aroma of breakfast enveloped me. My parents were in the kitchen, chatting excitedly.

"Isn't it wonderful?" my mom beamed, pouring milk over her cereal. "I'm so proud of Tommy for being true to himself! It takes so much courage."

"I know," my dad nodded thoughtfully. "It's great that he feels safe enough to tell you. We should really make sure he knows he has our support."

I sat down at the table, the clattering of cereal and spoons filling the air. My heart felt a mixture of happiness for Tommy and a tinge of anxiety about school. They were so excited that I couldn't help but feel the warmth radiating from them. It was odd, though. Here they were, celebrating Tommy's bravery, and meanwhile, I was battling my own shadows. Last year had been a tough ride, riddled with bullying that had dragged me down into a dark place I was still trying to pull myself out of.

"Yeah, it's amazing," I said, forcing a smile.

"Tommy's really great." My parents exchanged glances, and I could sense their unspoken concern. They cared, but they didn't truly understand the demons I faced, however they tried to support as much as they could.

We chatted about trivial things, and for a moment, I felt a sense of normalcy. I used to dread mornings like this, but today was different. There was no pressure, no schedule hanging over me like a dark cloud. The weight of school was still there, looming in the distance, but I decided to embrace today as an opportunity to reset.

As I finished my cereal, Flo texted me back a simple "Good morning! Can't wait to see you later!" I felt a spark of hope. I had nothing planned except some time to collect my thoughts. I could write, read, or maybe head to the park. The world felt a little lighter today.

After breakfast, I grabbed my journal and notebook. Sitting in my room with my thoughts was much better than facing the outside world just yet. I began to write, pouring everything onto the pages the struggles, the fears, the laughter, and the joy I felt for Tommy. Writing felt cathartic, a way for me to channel my emotions and fears into something tangible.

As I scribbled about Tommy's bravery, I realized how much I admired him. If he could share his authentic self, maybe I could learn to be more open about my struggles, too. I didn't have to carry the weight of the world alone. I could find my own courage, just like he did.

Time seemed to flow differently in the sanctuary of my thoughts. Today, I would set my fears aside and take it step by step. The road to healing was long, but every small moment of kindness, whether towards myself or others, was a step in the right direction. I was learning that it was okay to struggle and seek support, just as it was for Tommy. I might still have a long way to go, but for now, I was ready to embrace the journey.

The sun hung high in the sky, filtering through the curtains of my room, casting gentle patterns on the carpet. At that moment, however, all I could see were the endless notifications flickering on my phone screen. Social media felt like a double-edged sword; while it connected me to friends, it also brought back vivid memories of last year the relentless bullying, the sneers in the hallways, and the whispered taunts that echoed in my mind long after school was over. The thought of returning to that environment sent waves of anxiety crashing over me, and I could feel my heartbeat quicken, spiralling into a familiar panic.

Just as I sank deeper into despair, I heard the soft, tentative footsteps of my mother approaching. She had an innate ability to sense my emotional turmoil. Without saying a word, she knocked softly and opened the door, her warm presence filling the room. She didn't need to ask about my well-being; the distress on my face said it all. Instead, she simply sighed, concern etching her features. Then, with a swift determination born from love, she took out her phone and called Flo.

Florence was my anchor, my guiding light through the storm. As soon as I heard the familiar sound of her voice on the other end of the line, a flicker of hope ignited within me. Within minutes of her sprinting from her house, I could hear her hurried footsteps racing up the stairs. The instant she stepped into my room, time seemed to freeze. Her warm eyes searched for mine, and the concern etched on her face melted away the tumult in my mind.

"Hey, are you okay?" she asked gently, already wrapping her arms around me in an embrace that felt like coming home. I buried my face in her shoulder, and a fresh wave of tears escaped as I felt the weight of my fears start to lift. We slowly sank down to the floor, her arms enveloping me as if shielding me from the world outside.

"I'm scared," I admitted, my voice muffled. "What if it happens again?"

The memories crashed over me, each one a reminder of pain and loneliness. But she held me tighter, whispering soothing words that wrapped around me like a warm blanket.

"I'm here," Flo said softly, her voice calm and steady. "You're not alone. We'll face it together."

As I cried, her fingers brushed through my hair, and I could feel my racing heart begin to synchronize with the rhythm of her breathing. The panic that had threatened to consume me started to fade, replaced by the grounding force of her love.

Eventually, the sobs receded, and we shared a long, lingering kiss one that communicated everything words couldn't express. It was as if the world outside vanished, leaving just the two of us cocooned in our safe space. My mother watched quietly from the doorway, a small smile on her face. She could tell that Flo was more than just a girlfriend; she was the balm to my wounds.

As we pulled away, I felt the warmth of hope creeping back into my heart. Perhaps the journey ahead wouldn't be easy, but with Flo by my side, I believed I could face anything. The shadows of the past would always linger, but now I had someone to light the way forward. Together, we would turn the page, ready to embrace whatever the new school year would bring. With Flo's unwavering support.

A few moments ago, panic had gripped my chest like a vise; now, the storm had subsided, and my breaths were steady again, thanks to Flo.

She sat beside me, her arms wrapped tightly around my shoulders, anchoring me in a reality that felt safe. I buried my face in her shoulder, taking comfort in the warmth of her presence. Her scent a mix of lilac shampoo and the sweet hint of vanilla from the lotion she always used filled the air, soothing my frazzled nerves.

"You okay?" she asked softly, running her fingers through my hair.

I nodded but felt the need to share the chaos in my head. "I'm just... scared, you know?" My voice trembled slightly. "The new school year is starting soon, and I just can't shake off the fear that the bullying will come back. I don't want to go back to that dark place."

Flo tightened her embrace, a gesture filled with understanding. "You're not alone this time, though," she reassured me. "You have me, and Tommy, we are not going anywhere."

I met her eyes, searching for a spark of hope. "What if they do start again? What if I go back into that black hole?"

Her brow furrowed slightly, but a mischievous grin broke through. "Well, if they do, I'll just bring a big flashlight and some ice cream to rescue you! I'll be your superhero."

I couldn't help but chuckle, even if only for a moment. "And what if they have lasers?"

She gasped dramatically. "Then I'll bring extra ice cream. And maybe a cape! Capes are good for deflecting lasers."

We both laughed, the sound lifting some of the heaviness that clung to the air. It was moments like these, between the laughter and the shared fears, that reminded me why I loved her.

"I really appreciate you, Flo," I said, my voice quieter now. "You mean so much to me."

I leaned in closer, and she met me halfway. Our lips connected in a long, sweet kiss that melted away our worries, if only for a moment. I felt the warmth of her love enveloping me, reinforcing the idea that I wasn't battling this alone.

From the doorway, my mother watched silently, her heart aching at the sight of her son struggling yet finding solace in the embrace of someone who cared so deeply. Tears welled in her eyes as she witnessed Flo's ability to bring me comfort. It pained her to see me like this, yet it also filled her with hope that perhaps I was finding my way back to the light.

As we broke the kiss, flo held my gaze. "See? You have people who love you. We'll face whatever comes next together."

My heart swelled with gratitude. With her at my side, maybe this time the black hole wouldn't seem so inviting. Maybe this time I could fight back.

"Together," I echoed, feeling fortified by her words.

Florence smiled, her confidence contagious. "Absolutely."

I glanced at my mother, who smiled through her tears, and in that moment, I understood that love had a way of breaking through the darkness a way of illuminating the path ahead, no matter how daunting it seemed.

The afternoon sun filtered through my window as I watched Flo walk down the path back to her house, her silhouette slowly disappearing into the golden light. The moment of her arms around me was still fresh in my mind, a warm cocoon wrapping me against the storm that had threatened to pull me under. Panic had gripped me tightly moments before, a suffocating vice. But she had been my anchor, murmuring sweet nothings and reminding me to breathe, grounding me with her presence in a way I never knew I needed.

Once the door clicked shut behind me, the solitude washed over me like a wave. The familiar walls of my room felt both comforting and confining, a double-edged sword. I made my way upstairs, the soft creaks of the wooden steps underfoot echoing the remnants of our laughter just moments ago. The thought of school looming ahead like a dark cloud filled my chest with dread again, but I pushed it aside. Flo's soothing words replayed in my mind: "You're stronger than this."

Settling into my bed, I grabbed my headphones from the nightstand and plugged them into my phone. Music flooded my ears a mix of gentle melodies and uplifting beats. It was like a balm for my frayed nerves. I closed my eyes, letting the sounds wash over me, each note easing the tension that lingered in my shoulders.

I picked up the book I'd started a few days ago, its pages slightly crumpled from where I had dropped it in my moment of panic. The story inside, an adventure about a group of friends battling their own fears in a fantastical world, felt oddly relatable. I found comfort in their struggles, a reminder that I was not alone in facing my own demons. I got lost in the characters, their bravery sparking a flicker of hope within me.

As I turned the pages, I felt my mind slowly untangle itself. I thought about Flo and the way her presence had transformed my panic into something more manageable. She wasn't just my girlfriend; she was my confidante, my protector in a world that often felt overwhelming.

I considered how lucky I was to have someone who understood my struggles and who refused to let me drown in them.

The hours slipped away unnoticed as I journeyed deeper into the book. The sunlight began to wane, casting shadows in my room, but the darkness felt less foreboding now. I felt a sense of determination rising within me. If those characters could face their fears, then maybe I could, too. School was an upcoming challenge, one that terrified me, but Flo's faith in me reminded me that I could handle it.

I put the book down and took a deep breath, letting the music linger in the background. With every inhale, I imagined filling my lungs with strength, and with every exhale, I let go of clinging worries. School was just one chapter in my life, not the entire story. I had the best co-author by my side, ready to help me pen the next pages.

As twilight crept in, I finally felt lighter. I knew there would be hard days ahead, but each new day could begin with hope. I closed my eyes again, letting the music guide me into a peaceful state, filled with hope and gratitude for what was yet to come.

Good night diary!

Day 23

BREATHE
ANXIETY
MISSiNG
PiECE
Confused

Day 25

The sunlight streamed through the thin curtains of my room, casting a warm glow that I wished would chase away the cold dread settling in my chest. I inhaled slowly, reminding myself that I was safe. The chaos of yesterday felt like an echo, still reverberating in my mind. My panic attack had swept through me like a storm, leaving me gasping for breath and desperately reaching for Flo's comforting embrace. Her calming presence had anchored me, a lighthouse in the dark, but now she was gone, and I was left to face the remnants of my anxiety alone.

After a moment, I plucked up the courage to check my phone, hoping for a cheerful text from Flo. There it was a simple "Good morning! I hope you have a great day! Can't wait to see you!" With a soft smile stretching across my face,

I replied, "Good morning, beautiful! Thank you for everything yesterday. I'm feeling a bit better today."

Breakfast that morning was a familiar routine a bowl of cereal, the sound of milk splashing, and my parents' casual chatter that seemed to float just above my head. I picked at the flakes, my stomach twisted in knots. Each bite took effort, and the thought of another school year filled with exams and the spectre of bullying loomed over me like a storm cloud.

"You okay, kiddo?" Dad asked, his brows furrowed with concern as he looked up from his newspaper.

"Yeah, just thinking about school starting again," I replied, forcing a shrug as if brushing it off. I didn't want him to worry; he had enough on his plate. But thoughts of last year loomed large in my mind, vivid memories of whispered taunts and laughter that felt far from friendly. My mental health had taken a nose dive then, and I feared this year would be no different.

"Just remember, you have your friends Tommy and Flo they'll be with you. You're not alone in this," my mom chimed in, her voice soft and reassuring.

I nodded, though anxiety twisted the truth of her words into a fraying ribbon of hope. It was true; Tommy had promised to stand by me, and Florence had become a steady source of strength, her love wrapping around me like a protective cloak. But could they really help me face the impending chaos?

After breakfast, I sat down at the cluttered desk in my room, scraps of paper and textbooks piled high like an avalanche waiting to collapse. The information sheet for upcoming classes sprawled before me, each line demanding an answer, each blank space like a judgment. My hands trembled as I glanced at the questions: Which subjects would I focus on? What were my goals for the year?

Just as I began to fill it out, my phone buzzed with a message. It was Tommy, a goofy meme attached that made me snort. His unwavering ability to lighten my mood never ceased to amaze me. "Ready for another year of chaos?" he texted, followed by a string of exaggerated emojis that made me laugh.

I typed back, "I want to be ready, but honestly, I'm terrified."

He replied almost immediately. "You'll be fine! I'll be right there with you. Plus, Flo's got your back, and we both know you're tougher than you think. Don't forget that!"

Taking a deep breath, I tried to steady my racing heart. His words were a balm, soothing some of the worry gnawing at my insides. Slowly, I picked up the pencil again, determined to face what lay ahead.

As I filled out the information, recognizing that this year was a chance for a fresh start, the warmth of Flo's embrace lingered in my memory, fortifying my resolve. Every tick of the pencil felt like one small step toward reclaiming my life. With each check mark, I looked forward to being in classes with Tommy and Flo, knowing we'd face the challenges together.

And while the spectre of exams loomed, I reminded myself of the most important lesson I had learned: It was okay not to be okay. I had people who cared, and I could reach out when the darkness crept in.

With that thought, I put the pencil down and sent Flo a text. "Want to hang out later? I could use some company."

Moments later, her reply came buzzing back, a bright spot in my day: "Absolutely! How about we meet up at the pond? I'll bring the fun!"

An unexpected smile crept across my face, the first real one of the days. Maybe, just maybe, this year could be different. With friends at my side and the love of my life cheering me on, I felt a flicker of hope igniting within me.

The warm sunlight filtered through the vibrant canopy of leaves above, dappling the path as I made my way to the pond. The gentle rustle of the wind and the quiet chirps of birds created a symphony of nature, easing my nerves a little. Today, I needed Flo's comforting presence more than ever. Thoughts swirled in my mind like falling autumn leaves—worries about school, the looming spectre of bullying, and my struggles with anxiety.

As I reached the pond, I spotted her. Flo was sitting on the edge of the bench, her shinny hair illuminated by the sun, creating an almost ethereal glow around her. The moment our eyes met, a wave of warmth rushed over me, washing away a fraction of the weight I carried. I quickened my pace, eagerness breaking through the clouds of my worry.

"Hey," I greeted, breathless with excitement and relief.

She stood, her face lighting up with a smile that always made my heart flutter. In an instant, I was wrapped in her embrace. The world faded away as we hugged tightly, her warmth enveloping me, her presence grounding me. I felt an innate expectation of comfort in her arms. When we finally pulled apart, I couldn't help but murmur, "I've missed you."

"I missed you too," she replied softly. Then, without waiting for an invitation, she moved closer, pressing a sweet kiss to my cheek.

Her lips lingered, her eyes searching mine as if they held the answers to my unvoiced fears.

Eventually, we settled onto the familiar wooden bench, the surface worn smooth from countless moments shared in each other's company. I took a deep breath, trying to steady the storm inside me.

"I...I wanted to talk about something," I began, my voice almost a whisper.

"What's on your mind?" Flo's expression shifted to one of concern, her brow furrowing slightly. It made my heart ache, knowing I was the cause of that worry.

"It's about school," I said, hesitating. "I can feel the bullying creeping back… It's like a shadow that never truly goes away. I thought I was stronger, but some days, it just gets to me." I felt a lump in my throat, emotion threatening to spill over.

Flo reached out, taking my hand in hers. Her fingers intertwined with mine, warm and reassuring. "You don't have to face it alone," she said, her voice low but steady. "I'm here. We can get through it together like we always do."

My heart swelled at her words, the simple promise of support. "I know, but…" I trailed off, apprehension flooding my thoughts. "It just feels so... heavy. I don't want to drag you down with me. You deserve better."

"Listen," she interrupted softly, tilting her head to catch my eyes. "You're not dragging me down. We all have battles, and I want to help you with yours. Your feelings matter they matter a lot to me.

You're so much stronger than you think. My life would not be this happy if it wasn't for you showing love, hope and just how to be myself"

Her unwavering faith in me was like a beacon in the darkness. I squeezed her hand, seeking solace in her grip. "I guess I've just been feeling hopeless," I admitted, a wave of vulnerability crashing over me.

"When you feel hopeless, I want you to remember where you've come from and how far you've already fought. You're resilient, and every time you stand up to those shadows, it makes you stronger," Flo encouraged, her voice wrapping around me like a soothing blanket.

I felt her warmth spreading through me, igniting a flicker of strength. Even in the depths of my struggles, with Flo by my side, I gravitated toward the hope she offered.

"Thank you for always knowing what to say," I said, my voice thick with emotion.

She smiled, her eyes bright. "I'll always be here for you, no matter what. Promise."

As the wind picked up, gentle waves lapped at the pond's edge, reflecting the golden hues of the setting sun. The moment was simple, yet somehow profound two souls intertwined, navigating life together. Whatever storms awaited us, we would face them hand in hand.

In that quiet afternoon at the pond, I realized I had a fighting chance. Perhaps the shadows would always linger, but I didn't have to let them consume me. Together, we would carve out a space of light even in darkness.

As the sun began to dip below the horizon, painting the sky in hues of gold and pink, the soft lapping of water and the gentle rustle of leaves around us created a serene backdrop, one that felt comforting amidst our recent struggles with mental health.

We spoke candidly about our feelings, the weight of anxiety, the darkness that sometimes crept in uninvited. As we exchanged words, I admired how the evening light caught the strands of her hair and made her eyes sparkle with a mixture of vulnerability and strength.

Suddenly, in a moment that felt both electric and natural, we leaned into each other. Our lips met softly at first, hesitant, but that quickly gave way to a more passionate embrace. I felt her fingers interlace with mine, and then an exhilarating rush of warmth spread through me as her hands began to explore, daringly venturing to places that made my heart race.

But just as the world around us seemed to fade away, reality came crashing back with the sound of a jingling dog collar. A woman walked by, oblivious to our moment, her dog pulling her along the path. Our lips parted instantly, cheeks flushed with a mix of surprise and embarrassment. The world around us regained its volume, and I could hear the soft chuckle of the dog and the rustling of the grass beneath its paws.

Flo and I exchanged wide eyes, a silent agreement passing between us. That bubble of intimacy had burst, leaving us feeling exposed under the fading light. We both burst into laughter, the tension melting away as we navigated the clumsy awkwardness that had suddenly filled the air. But beneath the laughter, I could see the embarrassment creeping in, and it wrapped around us like a chilly breeze.

"I guess this isn't the best place for… that," Flo said, biting her lip to suppress her amusement.

"No … no," I agreed, chuckling nervously. "Definitely a bit too public."

We spent a few moments regaining our composure, casting furtive glances in the direction the woman had gone. The embarrassment hung there briefly, a cloud that was quickly dispelled by the warmth of our earlier conversation and the fleeting thrill of our kiss.

As the golden light slipped away, casting longer shadows across the pond, we knew it was time to go home. "I'll see you tomorrow?" I asked, my voice unsteady yet hopeful.

"Definitely," Flo replied, her smile re-emerging. We stood up from the bench, lingering for just a moment, the air heavy with unspoken words. Our eyes met, and in them, I saw a reflection of the connection we shared beyond embarrassment, deeper than mere attraction.

With a lingering wave, we turned in opposite directions, each step taking us further away from that pond, that moment. But even as we walked home me through the quiet streets, and her along the path lined with trees I carried with me the warmth of that encounter, the promise of what could be.

That night, as I lay in bed, I replayed the events over and over. Despite the embarrassment, there was an undeniable spark between us. Perhaps this was the beginning of something new, a deeper intimacy forged through shared struggles and spontaneous moments of connection.

Good night diary

Day 26

I stood in front of my closet, anxiously tugging at the hem of my favourite sweater vest. To anyone else, it looked like a simple piece of clothing, but for me, it was that. It was a small shield against the reality of returning to school, where lessons felt like too much pressure and expectations often loomed overhead like storm clouds. I could feel that familiar dread settling into my stomach, yet today was different. Today was mine, and I fought to hold onto that feeling.

After much deliberation, I settled on a pair of well-worn jeans and an olive-green sweater vest that read, "Arcade King." It seemed like a fitting choice for spending the day at the arcade with my girlfriend, Flo, and our Tommy and Evie. The thought of bright lights, the sounds of laughter, and the rush of competitive gaming filled me with a flicker of excitement. I glanced at the clock and rushed downstairs, where the aroma of morning coffee and toast wafted through the air.

"Good morning!" I chirped, plopping down at the breakfast table where my parents were already seated, engrossed in conversation about work. I poured myself a bowl of cereal and let the moment envelop me the warmth of family, the laughter that occasionally erupted from my dad's corny jokes.

As I chewed on a mouthful, my mom cleared her throat and shared the news that my sister, Mary, would be coming to visit with her boyfriend later in the week.

"They're leaving for Australia, and they wanted to see everyone before they take off," my mom said with a smile.

I had missed Mary. We always shared secret laughter at late-night snacks or binge-watching our favourite shows. The thought of her brings a soothing wave, a welcome reminder that amidst the chaos, something stable and familiar remained.

With a nod to my mom, I finished breakfast and retreated back upstairs, eager to complete my look for the day. As I dug into my dresser for my favourite sneakers, my thoughts drifted again. How would school treat me this year? Would the pressure tighten around my chest again when I stepped into the classroom for the first time? Would my anxiety keep me from truly enjoying my time with friends?

I shook off the intrusive thoughts. Not today. I had a day of fun ahead of me.

Once fully dressed, I grabbed my phone and checked the time. My friends would be meeting at the arcade soon, and I could hardly contain my enthusiasm. Last-minute preparations included slapping on some deodorant, a spritz of cologne, and my trusty snapback. Stepping in front of the mirror, I took a deep breath. "You've got this," I whispered to myself.

As I bolted out of the house, the cool morning air whipped at my cheeks, a refreshing slap that momentarily cleared my mind of the swirling thoughts about school. I could still hear the echoes of laughter and excitement in my head, remnants of conversations I had shared with my friends on brighter days. We all needed this outing more than just a day at the arcade; it was a lifeline of joy amid the darker clouds hanging over my life. Once on the bus, I felt a sense of relief that could not worry about school just for the day.

The bus screeched to a halt, and I hopped off, scanning the parking lot until my eyes landed on the flickering neon sign of the arcade. I parted the doors and let the vibrant lights wash over me, momentarily pushing away the worries that haunted me. The sounds of cascading laughter, the blips of arcade machines, and the sweet smell of cotton candy wove together and created a comforting blanket around me.

As I entered, it didn't take long to find Tommy. He was in front of the claw machine, chin tipped upward in concentration, his blue hair reflecting the lights above. His eyebrows furrowed in determination, he gripped the joystick like it was a life or death matter, and I couldn't help but chuckle softly at him.

"What are you trying to grab this time?" I teased, approaching him.

"Just a plushie, a dinosaur one, if I can get it," he replied, his voice rising with excitement as he manoeuvred the claw. "So far, no luck, but I'm determined! I bet it would look perfect on your bed." The mention of my bed ignited a spark of warmth in my chest, a reminder of the simpler times when our group could laugh and talk without the weight of the world pressing down on us.

With a gentle nudge, I stood beside him. "Here, let me try," I offered, and he stepped back with a mock bow. I took a deep breath, steadying my hands. As I focused on the brightly coloured plushie swaying just out of reach, memories of last year's torment rushed back whispers in the hallway, the cruel laughter, the feeling of walking through school as if underwater. But today, I was determined to let those thoughts dissipate.

I paused, letting the cacophony of the arcade seep into my bones. I moved the joystick with purpose, feeling the motion become instinctive. With a deep breath, I pressed the button. The claw descended, perfectly positioned. It latched onto the dinosaur, and for a heartbeat, I felt a wave of hope. But just as quickly, the claw betrayed me, slipping from its grip and leaving the plushie hanging precariously above the rest.

"Ahh! So close!" Tommy lamented, but he was already laughing, shaking his head as I sighed theatrically. Just then, the doors swung open, and I saw Florence and her friend Evie enter, their presence immediately saturating the air with warmth. The tension from earlier began to loosen. If there was any good reason to celebrate despite everything, it was this group my eclectic family amongst chaos.

"Hey, did you guys win anything yet?" Flo piped up, her ponytail bouncing as she approached our little gathering. "I'll show you how it's done."

"Hi, I'm Evie, Florence and I have been friends since we could talk, our parents work together." Evie said in a friendly tone.

"That's the same as Tommy and I; only difference is our parents don't work together." I said laughingly.

With Tommy still clutching the joystick, our laughter floated around us as we played for what felt like hours. But each moment of joy was underscored with my underlying struggles. The school year loomed over me like a dark cloud, and with every game we played, I felt the weight of anxiety creeping back into my mind.

Eventually, after a flurry of rounds and winning a few small prizes mostly due to Tommy's relentless optimism the four of us made our way to the food court. I leaned in, sharing trivial tales, and attempting to bury the echoes of hurt that chased me. Tommy cracked jokes about the ridiculous flavours of sodas, and Flo teased Evie about losing track of his points. It felt surreal as if the whole world outside had faded away.

While we munched on our greasy pizza and shared the last remaining bits of our smoothies, I felt better and lighter. The kids that bullied me were distant shadows outside this bubble of happiness, unable to intrude on the joy we had built here today. Even so, the thoughts bubbled under the surface.

"Are you okay?" Tommy asked, catching my gaze as I became lost in thought. His concern was genuine, and I appreciated it for what it was a reminder that I wasn't alone in this, even when it felt all-consuming.

"Yeah, just... thinking about school." I sighed, pushing my worries aside. "Right now, I'm just happy to be here with you guys."

"As it should be!" he declared with his usual flair. "We're not letting any school hype ruin our fun today. Let's grab those tickets and try to win something amazing."

The sounds of laughter and the clatter of plates filled the air in the bustling food court of the arcade. The scent of melted cheese and pepperoni wafted through the atmosphere, mixing with the rhythm of a nearby racing game. My girlfriend Flo and I shared a large pizza, the gooey cheese stretching as we pulled apart a slice. Beside us, Tommy was engaged in a friendly debate about the best gaming console while Evie sat quietly, her slice untouched beside her.

Evie, Flo's long-time friend, was normally vibrant and lively, but today, she seemed distant. I noticed her gaze darting around as if she was trying to navigate a path through invisible obstacles. Tommy was too wrapped up in his conversation to notice, but Flo had a gentle way of observing, and she shifted her attention toward Evie.

"Hey, you okay?" Flo asked gently, her voice a soothing melody against the chaos of chatter. Evie hesitated, her hands fiddling with the edge of her plate.

"It's just... sometimes it gets overwhelming," she finally admitted, her voice barely above a whisper. "I don't know why I can't just eat like everyone else. It feels like my brain is a video game with too many levels, and I can't find my way to the finish line. I ... have... autism, I don't really like talking about it..."

Flo reached over, placing her hand on Evie's arm. "It's okay," she said softly, her eyes full of understanding. "We're here for you, autism is not an illness it's just something you live with, like a superpower."

Evie glanced at us, her expression a mix of relief and uncertainty. "I struggle with routine changes and crowds. Sometimes, I feel lost in my own head. It's frustrating," she confided, her voice trembling slightly. "I can be standing right here and still feel like I'm miles away from everyone."

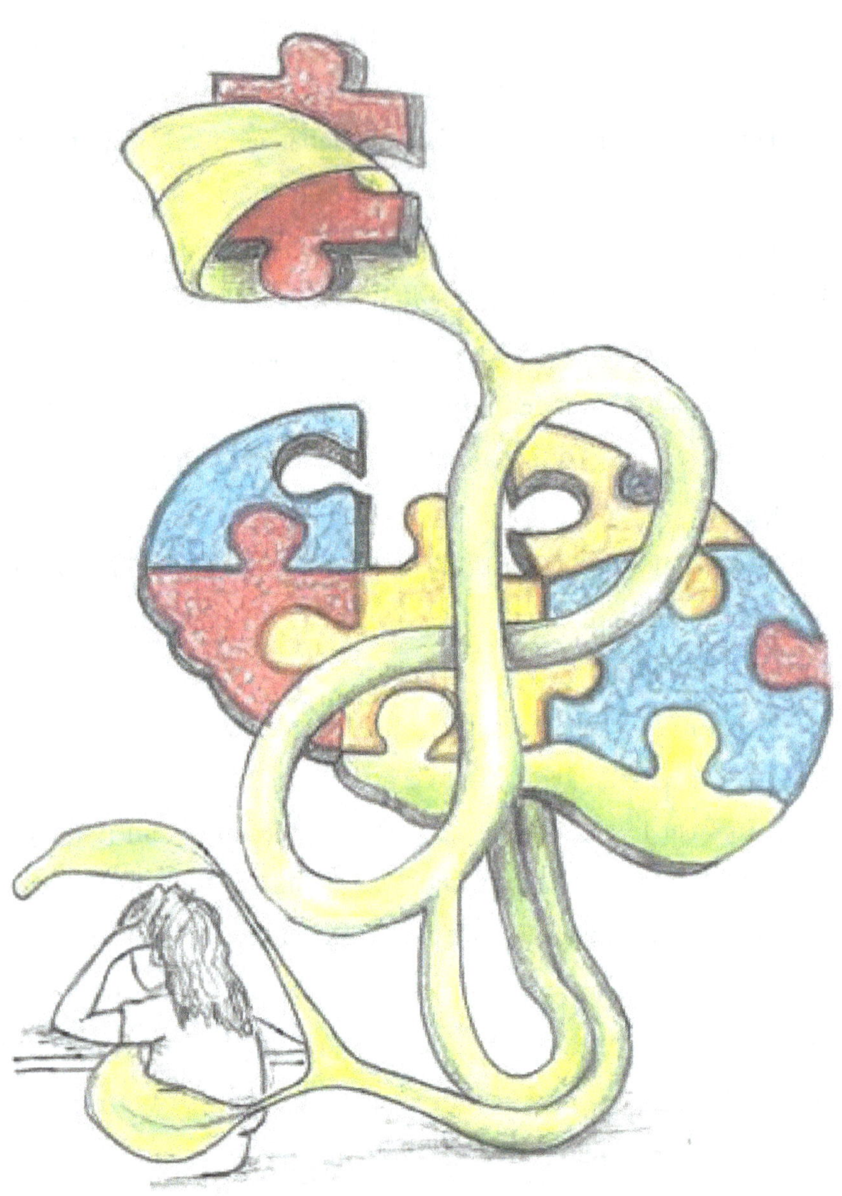

I could see the weight Evie carried, and it stirred something in me. My own struggles with mental health flashed through my mind those days when everything felt too heavy when the simplest tasks became monumental challenges. Gathering my courage, I leaned in closer, deciding to share a piece of myself.

"You know, Evie, I get that. I deal with anxiety a lot, too. There are times when I feel like I'm underwater, gasping for air while everyone else is swimming just fine. It helps to talk about it, though."

For a moment, her eyes widened in surprise, then softened. "Really?" she asked, a spark of connection igniting between us. "That makes me feel… not so alone."

"Exactly," I continued, relieved to see her smile for the first time that day. "Talking helps me feel less trapped. You're definitely not alone in this. We all have our battles, and that doesn't make you any less amazing."

Flo's smile radiated pride as she squeezed my hand tightly while kissing me on the cheek. "I'm really glad you shared that," she said, her voice warm and encouraging. "It's so important to speak about how we feel, especially with friends."

Evie's expression shifted, her cheeks flushing with a hint of colour as a smile broke through the clouds of her earlier discomfort. "You guys really understand, don't you?" she asked, a small grin peeking through.

"Of course," Tommy chimed in, finally catching on to the conversation. "We've all got our quirks and struggles. You're part of the team, Evie. We tackle life together, right?"

As we continued to talk, the once daunting food court transformed into a safe haven of acceptance and support. We reminisced about our favourite childhood games, shared dreams, and even cracked jokes about our gaming mishaps. The pizza between us slowly diminished as Evie finally took a tentative bite, savouring the flavours around her.

In that moment, alongside Flo, Tommy, and Evie, I realized that sharing our vulnerabilities wasn't a sign of weakness; rather, it was an act of bravery. With every word exchanged, the invisible walls began to crumble, revealing the strength of friendship forged through understanding. We may not have all the answers, but we had each other a tightly-knit team ready to face both the highs and lows together.4

The faint glow of neon lights flickered in the dimly lit arcade, reflecting the hazy joy that hung in the air. After devouring the last bites of pepperoni pizza, I felt a wave of contentment wash over me, especially with Flo nestled close. Tommy, ever the enthusiast, had suggested a round of air hockey, his eyes sparkling with excitement Evie naturally chimed in, eager for the competition.

We set up our teams: Flo and I teamed up against Tommy and Evie. The ribbing started immediately.

"You're going down!" Tommy declared, smirking as he adjusted his fake headband, the mini dinosaurs he had stuck all over it bobbing in rhythm with his confident swagger.

Flo giggled beside me, her laughter infectious. "Let's show them what we've got!" she said, pulling my arm playfully as we readied ourselves. So, the match began, a blur of hands swiping at the pucks, shuffling, and cheering. The scores didn't matter; it was all a chaotic tangle of laughter and friendly banter. Every time the puck whacked into the goal, we erupted in applause and dramatic gasps.

Yet, as the rounds progressed, it became clear: we were all equally terrible. Pucks drifted in elusive arcs, often ending up glancing off the edge of the table or disappearing altogether beneath the neon-lit chaos. Each failed shot was met with mock despair, and at one point, Tommy flopped dramatically onto the ground, clutching his heart.

"How can I go on?" he cried, eliciting a laughter rippling through the group.

Eventually, with our spirits high but our skills low, Tommy and Evie decided to venture off to try their hands at the claw machines again.

"You two should stay here and practice your game!" Evie teased, waving her hand dismissively as they ambled away.

Flo and I decided it was best to take a break too. The seating area beckoned a cosy alcove filled with oversized sofas, perfect for sinking into. We chose a corner couch, plush and inviting, and settled into its embrace. As we sat, I instinctively wrapped my arms around Flo, pulling her close as her head rested against my shoulder.

The world outside faded, the ambient sounds of competing games becoming a distant hum.

"How much fun was that?" Flo asked, her smile radiant. Our eyes met, and I saw in her gaze an understanding that made the weight I often carried feel a little lighter.

"Honestly? I haven't laughed like that in a while," I admitted, feeling a rush of warmth that had nothing to do with the arcade's vibrant atmosphere. "Sometimes, when I get caught up in my head, I forget how to just… enjoy moments like this."

Flo tilted her head, concern flickering in her eyes. "You know, you can talk to me, right? Whenever you're feeling overwhelmed?"

I nodded, the sincerity in her voice wrapping around my heart like a warm blanket. "I know. You help me a lot more than you realize," I said softly, grateful for her presence.

We sat in comfortable silence for a moment, the laughter of our friends a background melody. Then Flo broke it with a playful glint in her eyes. "Okay, enough serious talk. I want to know your air hockey strategy."

I chuckled, the mood lifting. "My strategy? Desperation, mostly. Maybe a dash of luck."

Another round of laughter bubbled over us, and as I leaned down to kiss her, I felt a tug in my chest, a lightness that reminded me of how much joy could be found in these simple moments. In that cosy corner of the arcade, surrounded by laughter and warmth, I realized that even amidst my struggles, there was beauty to be found in shared happiness.

When Tommy and Evie returned, grinning and bickering about who had won the last candy prize from the claw machine, it felt like everything was in perfect harmony. We all settled back into the games, trading playful jabs with each goal and enjoying the friendly competition.

And though I knew the complexities of my mental health journey wouldn't vanish in a day, sitting there with Flo, Tommy, and Evie, I felt the kind of joy that made it a little easier to bear. It was in the laughter, the playful banter, and the love I felt surrounding me.

The neon lights of the arcade flickered behind us as we stepped out into the cool evening air. The sounds of laughter and the beeping machines faded into the distance, replaced by the familiar rhythm of our footsteps on the pavement. Flo wrapped her arms around herself, her face a mixture of joy from the games and a tinge of sadness that I couldn't quite understand. Tommy, ever the cheerful spirit, nudged me with a grin that seemed to radiate positivity.

"What was your favourite game, Flo?" he asked, hoping to draw her attention back to the day's fun.

Her lips formed a small smile, but it didn't quite reach her eyes. "The racing game was cool," she replied, but it felt like there was something holding her back. We exchanged glances; both Tommy and I could sense that she wasn't okay.

"It's just Evie leaving, isn't it?" I said gently. She nodded, a hint of sadness clouding her vibrant blue eyes. I placed an arm around her shoulders, feeling the warmth of her presence against the chill of the evening. Tommy joined in, wrapping his arm around us both a comforting triangle of friendship.

"She'll be okay. We'll see her again," Tommy reassured, trying to lighten the mood. Flo leaned into me a little, her chin resting on my shoulder.

Once we reached the bus stop, the streetlights cast a soft glow as we waited. Evie was soon picked up by her mum, and as we waved goodbye, there was a sense of finality in the air. The bus rolled up, its tires creaking as we climbed aboard. We settled in the back, with Flo quietly looking out the window while Tommy animatedly recounted a funny moment from earlier.

As we stepped off the bus at our stop, I could feel Flo's reluctance to part ways. "You sure you don't want to hang out for a bit?" I offered as Tommy walked in the direction of his home.

"No, I think I just want to go home and relax," she said softly, biting her lip.

I reached out and gently cupped her face, pulling her closer. "Okay, but just know I'm here if you need anything." We shared a sweet kiss, one that felt both warm and heavy with unspoken words. After, she smiled faintly before turning to head home.

The familiar scent of home enveloped me as I stepped inside. My parents greeted me with casual chatter about their day, but as I shared the highlights of mine Flo, the arcade, and what I'd learned about Evie and her struggles with autism the atmosphere shifted. I could see the pride in my parents' eyes; they knew how much I cared for my friends.

Later that evening, I sank into my bed, my phone buzzing beside me. I was eager to talk to Mia again her laughter still echoed in my mind. But as the minutes turned into hours, and messages went unanswered, a knot formed in my stomach. Maybe she was tired or just spending time with her family. I decided to let it be and closed my eyes, letting the events of the day wash over me in a peaceful wave of exhaustion. The comfort of our moments together lingered, yet the shadows of her worries still loomed.

And so, as the night, the world outside continued its stillness, but in our hearts, the story was just beginning, waiting for the dawn to break with new understandings and deeper bonds. Good night diary!

Day 27

The sun filtered through the curtains, casting a soft glow across my room. I lay there, staring at the ceiling, my mind a swirl of anticipation and dread. Tomorrow marked the start of school an event that normally would have sent my anxiety skyrocketing. But this year felt different. I wasn't facing it alone. I had Florence and Tommy by my side, and after the amazing day we'd shared at the arcade yesterday, I thought maybe, just maybe, it would be alright.

But as I flipped my phone over and over in my hands, my heart sank a little more. Flo hadn't replied to my text. She always responded promptly, and her absence felt like a weight pressing down on my chest. Maybe she's just busy, I told myself repeatedly, trying to shake the growing worry.

After a long moment, I pushed the thought aside, deciding to treat today just like any other. I crawled out of bed and shuffled to my closet, pulling on a favourite sweater vest and a pair of jeans. As I stood in front of the mirror, I practiced a smile, reminding myself that whatever challenges lay ahead, I was not facing them alone.

The scent of pancakes wafted through the air, coaxing me down the stairs. My parents were already seated at the kitchen table, each absorbed in their morning routines. The chatter of the news in the background melded with the sound of silverware clinking against plates, a familiar comfort.

"Morning, sleepyhead," my dad greeted me with a grin. I forced a smile back and slid into my chair.

"Hey! How're you feeling about tomorrow?" my mom asked, her eyes searching mine for any hint of unease.

"Terrified," I admitted, the word escaping my lips before I could stop it. "But I've got Flo and Tommy with me this year." Saying their names brought a flicker of warmth to my chest, a reminder that I wasn't alone.

"Well, that's good!" my mom replied, her tone lightening the mood. "It makes a big difference to have friends. What about Florence? Is she ready for school?"

I hesitated, once again reminded of her silence. "I don't know. She hasn't replied to my text from last night," I confessed. It felt strange to voice my concern out loud, but I knew Mom would understand.

My dad shrugged a fatherly nonchalance. "Maybe she's busy getting ready. School prep can be overwhelming, you know?"

I nodded, trying to push the worry further down. After all, I had no reason to believe anything was wrong; Flo could just be tangled up in her own world, getting ready for the year ahead. I focused again on my parents, enjoying the warmth of their presence and the comfort of a good breakfast.

As I chewed on my pancake, I recalled yesterday's adventure, the bright lights of the arcade, the thrill of competing with Tommy in pop-a-shot, and the laughter that echoed throughout the hall. Flo's bright smile as she emerged victorious from a game, the way her laughter rang like bells in the air. It made the tension in my chest ease just a little. I wanted more days like that, filled with joy and support.

After breakfast, I savoured a few more moments with my parents, then returned to my room to keep busy. I organized my backpack, laying out everything I might need for the first day new notebooks, freshly sharpened pencils, the courage I would need to face whatever was coming.

Just as I finished, my phone buzzed. My heart raced as I grabbed it, hoping it was an incoming message from Flo! I clicked it open, and my breath held in anticipation, however, it was Tommy.

"Hey! I'm just checking in to see if you are okay with tomorrow. I've had a crazy day getting ready and helping my little brother with stuff. I can't wait to see you tomorrow!"

"I am really scared, but I have people with me this year and I have you, I should ask you how are you feeling going into school... as your... true self|". I replied.

"I have never felt worried about what people will say and think, anyway, how is Flo feeling". Tommy texted.

"I don't know she has not replied since the arcade yesterday." I texted back.

"she is probably getting ready for a busy school year ahead", he replied.

"that is what my parents said, I have to finish getting my stuff ready, talk later" I texted.

The butterflies in my stomach danced with a mix of excitement and anxiety as I glanced at the calendar. My mental health had been taking small steps towards improvement, and I had Flo and Tommy at my side, lifting me in ways I hadn't anticipated.

Just yesterday, we'd spent an incredible day at the arcade, laughter mingling with the sound of flashing lights and the cacophony of excited voices. I could still hear the ring of the games echoing in my mind the, the thrill of winning a round of air hockey against Tommy, and the way Flo's eyes sparkled when she won a giant stuffed bear from the claw machine, which she insisted on naming "Fuzzy." Everything felt perfect then, and I walked home feeling like I was finally finding my place in the world.

But now, my smile faded as I scrolled through my messages, trying to reach Flo. She hadn't replied to my texts or picked up any of my calls. I felt an uneasy knot tighten in my stomach as I stared at the screen, hoping for a response. It wasn't like her to leave me hanging.

"Make sure you get your things sorted for school tomorrow," my mum called out from the other room, her voice pulling me back into the moment. I could hear the sound of clothes being folded and the rustle of notebooks being stacked.

"I'm just going to Flo's to see if she's okay," I replied, trying to keep the tremor out of my voice.

My mum looked up, her brow furrowed slightly with concern. "Okay, but not for long. You need to finish getting sorted."

I nodded, though I was already halfway out the door, my heart pounding in rhythm with my footsteps as I walked to Flo's house. The late afternoon sunlight cast long shadows on the pavement, but I hardly noticed. All that occupied my mind was a swirling mix of worry and dread. None of my mental health mattered at this moment in my life. Each hesitant knock on her door echoed in my head, a heightened crescendo of anxiety.

When her parents answered I said, "Is Florence ok because she is not answering my texts or calls.".

They seemed taken aback. "She's not here? I thought she was having a sleepover at yours," they said.

"Wait, what?" I replied, confusion flooding my mind. "I asked her to hang out yesterday after the arcade, but she said she wanted to get home. I haven't seen her since the bus last night."

The worried look on her parents' faces mirrored me. They turned anxiously to each other, whispers passing between them as the heavy atmosphere settled over us.

"We need to find her," I said, the urgency in my voice unmistakable.

"Let's try calling her again," her mom suggested, pulling out her phone, and I followed suit. Calls went unanswered, and voicemails were left without a single reassuring sign of life.

As time passed, the light began to dim, and the worry morphed into something heavier an ominous cloud enveloping me. We all felt it, three worried hearts racing under the weight of uncertainty.

We decided to search her favourite places, parks, the coffee shop she loved, and even the arcade where we'd spent the day before. With each place we found empty, my heart sank deeper into despair. Was she hurt? Did something happen on the way home? Each thought spiralled deeper until anxiety felt like a crushing weight on my chest.

We started to reach the pond where we first said I love you to each other. I have never felt so scared or worried like this before. The person I love and care the most about is missing! What do I do? Flo's dad and I reached the pond,

I found her bracelet on the floor, the one she would never take off and the one she loved playing with. This sent me in a spiral and it made me think of the worst.

"Hey, look I found her bracelet she must be close" I yelled at the top of my lungs.

Her father hugged me, and we both started to break down in tears, thinking what had happened while grabbing the bracelet and holding it tight.

"Florence... Flo... Florence!" he screamed while holding his tears back.

"Where are you, please just come back, we can help with anything" I cried out.

Slowly, we both collapsed to the ground, and our minds just thought the worst had happened.

My mind just kept thinking only about what has happened, and I just wanted to hug her and tell her she was right, but my mind was like a roller-coaster as I broke down.

What has happened to the one person I could say anything to, she was my peace, love and guidance.?

Mental Health is a person's overall emotion and mental well being, it's an important part of a person's life. Its more than just the absence of mental illness and it can happen to anyone at any stage in their lifetime.